Discovered

The Collector Series

Discovered

Ali Whippe

4 Horsemen
Publications, Inc.

Discovered
Copyright © 2022 Ali Whippe. All rights reserved.

4 Horsemen
Publications, Inc.

4 Horsemen Publications, Inc.
1497 Main St. Suite 169
Dunedin, FL 34698
4horsemenpublications.com
info@4horsemenpublications.com

Cover by Valerie Willis
Typesetting by Autumn Skye
Edited by Sienna Skye

All rights to the work within are reserved to the author and publisher. No part of this publication may be reproduced, stored in a retrieval system, or transmitted in any form or by any means, electronic, mechanical, photocopying, recording, scanning, or otherwise, except as permitted under Section 107 or 108 of the 1976 International Copyright Act, without prior written permission except in brief quotations embodied in critical articles and reviews. Please contact either the Publisher or Author to gain permission.

This book is meant as a reference guide. All characters, organizations, and events portrayed in this novel are either products of the author's imagination or are used fictitiously. All brands, quotes, and cited work respectfully belong to the original rights holders and bear no affiliation to the authors or publisher.

Library of Congress Control Number: 2022936705

Paperback ISBN-13: 978-1-64450-603-5
Audiobook ISBN-13: 978-1-64450-602-8
Ebook ISBN-13: 978-1-64450-604-2

Dedication:

For Valerie Willis…

Thanks for letting me enjoy some time with Tony!

Contents

Chapter 1 1
Chapter 2 12
Chapter 3 23
Chapter 4 37
Chapter 5 47
Chapter 6 54
Chapter 7 63
Chapter 8 76
Chapter 9 82
Chapter 10 90
Chapter 11 99
Chapter 12 112
Chapter 13 120
Chapter 14 129

Chapter 1

Dinner and a review of the rules

"A few reminders," Amberleigh tells the vampire sitting across from her, "before we get started tonight." They have eaten a lovely dinner, enjoyed a luscious dessert, indulged in a respectable amount of wine, and settled the no doubt enormous bill. The time has come to discuss business.

Lucard gives her a long look with his deep green eyes, the vampire pushing her with his power, insisting she move forward without the bother of such details. Amberleigh feels the compulsion spill off him like a cloud, the force of his desire warring with her free will. Her succubus power perks up at the possibility of so much energy, but she pushes it back down easily. This is not her first time dealing with vampires—hence, the rules.

Discovered

She gives her dinner companion a hard kick under the table, the tip of her heel doing more damage to his perfectly ironed pant leg than to his actual body and offers a wide smile. "Stop," she orders, "or the entire deal is off."

"You are so serious." Lucard frowns, rolling his eyes and running a pale hand through his shaggy brown hair. He's dressed like any wealthy man taking a date out to a fancy restaurant: white button-down shirt, thin black tie, dark suit jacket, clearly tailored for his swimmer's physique. Amberleigh hasn't seen him naked yet, but she knows the type. His underwear, if he wears any, probably has a designer label, and if he is like the other vampires she's worked with, he's probably wearing a corset to keep his waistline tight. Some vampires never really let go of the fashion trends popular when they were alive—and Lucard strikes her as particularly vain.

This isn't a problem for Amberleigh. She doesn't mind vanity. She also doesn't mind the copious amount of money he has agreed to pay her in exchange for her services tonight. But she does mind his attitude right now, the pompous way he just tried to charm her.

I can't wait for him to spend some time as a human, she thinks, smiling brightly at him. *It will do him some good. Maybe someone will hurt him just a little, remind him of what it's like to be powerless.*

Dinner And A Review Of The Rules

Lucard returns her smile with a charm that isn't entirely due to his supernatural abilities, the look making his handsome face practically glow, and she recants. *I don't mean that. I don't wish him ill. He's just ... a vampire who doesn't know how to live without his powers. That's why he found me.*

"Now," she says, beginning her reminder speech again, "the rules, Lucard."

"Rules," he scoffs, the century he spent in France obvious in the sound. "They are meant to be broken."

Amberleigh laughs. "Says the vampire planning to be human for the next three days. Are you sure you know what you're getting into?"

"I'm sure I can survive a mere few days," Lucard says flippantly. "Being human isn't all that difficult."

"No?" she prompts, leaning forward to peer at him. "Then why do you need me?"

He narrows his eyes at her, and she feels that push of power again, dangerously close, but he restrains himself this time, not imposing his will upon her. She could use her own powers of seduction to distract and calm him, but she doesn't, waiting instead to see what he will do next. She wonders how much control he has over his abilities — a hint of what she can expect from tonight. He leans in closer, that handsome mouth curling as he speaks the warning. "Watch yourself, little

Holder, lest your abilities make you careless with your words."

"We're still having this conversation because I am not careless," she reminds him, pushing back just as hard. "Now, again, tell me the rules."

Lucard sighs but holds his hand out, lifting a finger for each point. His nails are perfectly manicured. Amberleigh studies his hands, wondering how they will feel on her skin, before rallying and returning to the conversation. He's only humoring her, but she still needs him to say it, to assure herself that this time will be different.

Everything will work out fine.

"The payment is delivered up front and is non-refundable, regardless of the experience I have. The contract begins when we leave here," he pauses, licking his lips, "with a kiss and expires in 72 hours when we meet at your apartment, and I reclaim my powers." This time, there is no mistaking the heat in his eyes as he pauses, then adds, "With the best sex of your life."

Amberleigh rolls her eyes, like she hasn't heard that one before, but nods, gesturing for him to continue. When he doesn't speak, she says, "And the final rule?"

"You don't need to worry about it," he insists. "I have no plans to die tomorrow."

"Well, I have no plans to spend the rest of my nights as a vampire," she snaps, "so show

Dinner And A Review Of The Rules

up on time to take it back, or we will have a problem."

"No problem," he assures her, then narrows his gaze, cocking his head to the side as he examines her. "Why are you doing this?"

"Because you're paying me a lot of money," she replies, thinking of the house she has seen online, the small porch and the open ocean under the sun halfway across the world.

He shakes his head. "Yes, but why now?" He looks around the restaurant, nodding at the tasteful seasonal decorations, the red pillar candle in the center of table, the poinsettias in the corner of the room, the tree in the distant lobby. "You need a distraction for the holiday? Feeling sentimental, little succubus?"

Amberleigh laughs, shaking her head. "I need another house for the holiday," she answers honestly, "a little gift for myself, and your proposal arrived at the perfect time."

"You are leaving the city?" Lucard asks. He sounds genuinely offended at the prospect.

"Oh god no," she says quickly. "But I found the perfect little place on the Med, and I need it in my life. Helping you out right now gets me another vacation home." She sees the interest in his eyes, but the vampire does not ask about her properties. He probably already knows about most of them, definitely the penthouse in the city and the cottage upstate. She keeps several residences, using the ones that correspond to the creature in question.

Discovered

Vampires love the city, so they are easy enough to please—and Amberleigh loves having a doorman. Werewolves need open space and no neighbors, so her property outside the city suits those encounters. She has an indoor pool at the house out in Long Island, so the water fae can choose their pleasure, the converted boarding school in Millbrook for the witches who appreciate dramatic flair and access to ley lines, and the small house in Brooklyn for those who don't want to be spotted in Manhattan. She thinks her walk-up in Midtown might still be her own secret, but she doesn't mind too much if it isn't. The creatures won't try to harm her—she provides a valuable service to the community. Also, she can disarm them with a kiss, so it's not like she's helpless.

She watches the vampire across the table, imagining what her night with him will be like. Definitely worth the money—and the intrusion into her personal life. Lucard wouldn't have contracted her without looking into all aspects of her life as well as relying on her reviews in the supernatural community. He steeples his hands below his chin, narrowing his gaze. "Do you not have loved ones that you want to see for the holiday?"

Amberleigh ignores the probing nature of the question, letting the vampire pry deeper into her personal life. No doubt he already knows that her brother Benjamin works as a

Dinner And A Review Of The Rules

consultant to the wealthy on Wall Street, that their parents died in a car accident three years ago, that she's been working as a Holder since she was twenty.

"Because all humans care about Christmas? Maybe I'm Jewish." She raises an eyebrow. "I can ask you the same: do you want to be human on Christmas for nostalgia or are you meeting someone's family tomorrow and want to avoid eating their adorable nephew?"

She cocks her head, sizing up what she already knows about him: Lucard de Monteban has been a vampire since 1748, originally from Eastern Europe, and after spending a century and a half on the continent, he emigrated to the New World at the start of the 20th century. He is known for his integrity among creatures and humans alike and his dedication to helping the less fortunate—as long as he also benefits in the long run. As a vampire, he can afford to wait for the very long run, and he is responsible for at least two shelters in the city that are still thriving—both run by churches: Catholic and Presbyterian.

Watching his non-reaction to her guesses, she tried a different angle. "Are you just longing to hear Midnight Mass in Latin again? You know it's broadcasted on TV, right? Or do you miss the sunrise and can't wait until after New Year's?" She touches on both of the vampire's weaknesses—inaccessible holy ground and deadly sunlight.

Lucard's face darkens, the connection they had been sharing a moment earlier fading, and his voice is quiet when he speaks. "My reasons are my own."

So it's either the church thing or the sun thing—and I'm betting the former. She could follow him after they part tonight and see for sure, but she doesn't really care about his reasons. Lucard is convenient, a solid client, and pleasant to look at. She's looking forward to seeing what three hundred years of practice has done to his abilities in bed.

Shrugging, she reaches around to pull the black wrap on the back of her chair up and over her shoulders again, covering the black cocktail dress she wears as she prepares to leave. "Very well," she assures him, giving an inviting smile. "You don't owe me an explanation." She reaches for her clutch, then raises an eyebrow at him expectantly. "Are you ready?"

He closes his eyes for a moment, his shoulders lifting as he takes a breath, no doubt readying himself for the loss of the vampirism he has lived with for centuries, then nods. His green gaze meets hers, and he stands up, taking her hand and leading her out of the restaurant. They collect their coats in the lobby, Amber stowing her tiny purse in a deep coat pocket, then walk slowly outside together, hand in hand.

Dinner And A Review Of The Rules

The frigid New York air bursts over their exposed skin as they reach the street, and Amberleigh leans into him, using his taller frame to block the worst of the wind. He leads her down the block, crossing the next street and heading to the park. They had discussed the best place for the transfer, and Lucard insisted that he wanted to see her face in the moonlight of Central Park when she first looked at the world through vampire eyes. She reminded him that he was not the first vampire she has Held for—though she did not tell him that he is only the third. He warned her that his power would be different; after all, he was older than her previous lovers.

He isn't, but she didn't tell him that. For all that she knows about Lucard de Monteban, she isn't sure how he would react if she told him that nine years ago, when she was just starting her career, she held for Gerard Valentine, the oldest and most powerful vampire in the New York area, for over a week. Gerard is a different kind of vampire, ruthless and brutal, and Amberleigh isn't proud of her time with him, the way his power had left her empty and desperate, needing more of his attention for the next weeks until she could wean herself away.

She hadn't Held for vampires for five years after that, not until her parents died and she wanted to feel powerful for a moment—plus, it bought the apartment in Manhattan

Discovered

and paid the fees for the next few years. Holding for vampires is dangerous. Their power affects her for days afterward—not to mention the risk if something happens to the vampire while she holds their abilities. Amberleigh isn't kidding with her rules—her contract demands that she be paid ten times the original agreement if something happens to the vampire during their agreement. She does not want to spend the rest of eternity as a bloodsucker—but if it happens, at least she won't have to keep working.

Maybe I'll do it for free then, she muses. *I will still have to keep myself entertained on the long, lonely nights.* She wonders idly if she were to retain the vampire's powers eternally if she would continue to work as a Holder, absorbing other creature's powers as well.

You know you can.

She stops the line of thought immediately, wiping Odo from her mind completely, never certain if vampires could actually read minds or if their long experience just allowed them to be really perceptive about human desires.

You haven't thought about Odo in years. Stop thinking about him now. This is not the time.

She looks up at her vampire companion, getting herself back in the moment as she admires the line of his jaw, the way his hair blows in the windy night, pressing up against the black hat he put on when they walked outside. She wishes she had brought a hat,

Dinner And A Review Of The Rules

but she also knows how much Lucard loves the way her blonde hair rushes around her face, tendrils blown loose from her chignon framing her rosy cheeks. Her coat is warm enough, and the tights she wears are actually lined for the cold—a clever product she discovered that looks like thin black stockings but is warm and cozy. The flat-bottomed boots are a nod to fashion as well as practicality—it has been a week since the last snow, but the sidewalks still have patches of ice here and there. Amberleigh likes to have her feet steady beneath her, especially when she is preparing to leap into new powers.

Chapter 2

A walk in the park

Lucard leads them into the park but not very far under the dark trees. He is aware that he will be leaving as a human—and he doesn't want to tempt any muggers on his first night. Amberleigh need not fear any humans on her way home; she will be strong with vampire powers. She will probably have to feed from someone before she sees Lucard again. The idea causes a shiver to run down her back. The first time she Held for a vampire, she killed someone in her need—a man who didn't run when she told him to leave her alone. This time, she thinks she should be able to restrain herself and stop before the heart does. She has practiced a lot of yoga and meditation in the last few years—mastering her control over her desires as she learned control over her body. And Lucard may be old, but he's not as strong as Gerard, so the need shouldn't be so overwhelming.

Even so, she hopes the enormous fee and the new vacation home will soothe her guilty conscience if anything does happen.

They make their way along the path, heading for an underpass cloaked in darkness. Amberleigh reaches out with her senses as they approach, making sure no other beings—human or creature—are nearby. Her succubus abilities allow her to sense other beings when she concentrates, getting a sense of the power contained within the person in question–a way to judge suitable partners. Over the years since her gift manifested, Amberleigh has learned to identify certain creatures by feel along with stronger humans who can last the night with her. Right now, they share the underpass with two tiny creatures, likely rats, and no one else. As they pass underneath and into the darkness, Lucard presses her against the wall, leaning down to sniff her neck, nuzzling between her scarf and the collar of her coat, seeking skin. His breath is warm on her chilled skin, and she shivers, leaning back to give him access. She knows he won't bite her. That's not until Thursday night when he reclaims his abilities. His hands work at the buttons of her coat, freeing them instantly, and then his hands are sliding against her hips, one snaking around to press her back while the other squeezes her ass. The cold air rushes in, but she doesn't mind, enjoying his touch. His hand moves from her ass to her front, brushing between her legs, hitting the mark through her thick tights. She moans a little, opening her eyes to look at him. He is watching her face, enjoying the pleasure he can give her.

"You know that's not how this works," she reminds him, sensing the rising tide of his desire, the need for more immediate satisfaction. "Not unless you only want to spend a few moments as a human before it's all over."

"Maybe I just like the noises you make," he murmurs, leaning down to kiss her neck. His mouth is warm, his lips soft, and little fires erupt under her skin despite the chilly air. *Oh yeah,* she thinks, *a few centuries of practice definitely make a difference.*

"I can't wait to make all the noises you enjoy," she says breathily, always loving this part of the encounter, the moments before the exchange, when she is still a human woman being pleasured by a supernatural creature — well, as human as she ever gets. She can feel her own power rising, the magic in her ready to drain the magic from her companion, but she holds it back, waiting for the moment to set it free. Lucard kisses her neck again, his hands moving to run up her sides and cup her breasts. He leans away, diving below her scarf this time to kiss the exposed skin of her chest.

A Walk In The Park

Her gold necklace is cold against her skin in the night air, the small medallion leaving a circle of ice against her skin. She wore her mother's necklace tonight, knowing that her traditional silver necklace would burn the vampire if he touched it—and eventually it will burn her after she absorbs his powers—along with his weaknesses.

Lucard leans away, meeting her eyes with a meaningful gaze. "You wear powerful magic, little Holder," he whispers. "I can feel the soul magic in that medallion."

"Family heirloom," she replies, not wanting to think about her mother while a sexy vampire is kissing her chest. "Long sordid history."

"You shall have to tell me more of this sordid history," he croons, leaning back down to kiss the other side of her chest, then moving deftly around her scarf to kiss up her neck. "Later," he promises, "when I have you in my bed."

Amberleigh doesn't remind him that they will be in her bed for the immediate future—she doesn't meet lovers in strange places, and it would take a long time for her to trust the vampire enough to stay at his place. Amberleigh may enjoy encounters with random strangers, but she always sets the terms—her place, her rules, her limits. Her Holder abilities keep her safe, but in the world of the supernatural, her succubus abilities are a small power. A stronger creature could hold her captive if they really wanted to—especially if she couldn't get close enough for a kiss. She doesn't want to tempt anyone to try, feeling superior with the succubus at their mercy.

She considers the vampire caressing her now. Lucard is stronger, easily able to overpower her if he chose, but he is also under her thrall, enticed by her succubus powers that have wrapped him in desire. Also, he needs something from her, so he won't hurt her. Not while he entrusts her with his own power. Vampires aren't complex creatures—not like the fae. She can relax and enjoy herself here. Lucard's mouth lingers at the line of her jaw, trailing small kisses in a line of fire across her skin, before he leans back to look in her eyes again.

Amberleigh rallies, calling herself back to the moment and trying to ignore the thrill in her body at the promise in the vampire's touch. *It's time*, she tells herself.

"Ready?" she asks, the word barely escaping her lips. The vampire nods, then without a pause, claims her lips with his own. He is a skilled kisser, his mouth moving expertly against hers, but Amberleigh barely notices.

She never really feels that first kiss, too absorbed by the sensation of her power reaching out and washing over them both. It starts small enough, a rush of strength in her arms and legs, a tingle along her skin as

A Walk In The Park

her nerves roar to life, and then a burst of awareness as his immortality sinks into her. She keeps her eyes closed, the assault on her other senses enough for the moment. She can hear everything: the scurrying of rats in the darkness, the wind in the branches of the trees beyond their shelter, the murmur of distant voices from the street, the rumble of traffic, a distant horn, and the distinctive clop of horse hooves on pavement from the carriages at the edge of the park. The former vampire holding her ends the kiss, releasing her slowly. His hands slide down her sides, the motion making her skin break into eager goosebumps, and he steps away from her. His fingers merely brush against the fabric of her dress, but Amberleigh hears each strand being touched, the sound like a flag snapping in a brisk wind. She can hear each breath he takes and the slow steady thump of his newly beating heart.

Another hunger creeps along her skin at the realization, and she opens her eyes, staring at the former vampire as he watches her. His newfound breath catches, and he raises a hand to his chest. "You," he says simply.

"Me," she echoes, marveling at the sound of her voice in her new ears, the tones layered and melodic in a way she has never heard before.

"You are…" he pauses, taking another steadying breath, relishing the need to breathe, "breathtaking."

She chuckles, admiring the simple ordinariness of the man before her. As a vampire, Lucard is hypnotic, the kind of man who attracts attention from across the room; as a man, he is handsome and confident but not remarkable beyond that. No one would ever kick him out of bed, but he isn't likely to haunt anyone's dreams. "So that's what you look like," she says quietly, still analyzing the depth of her own voice.

"How do I look?" he asks, reaching up to trace a finger down her cheek.

"Normal," she breathes, every part of her being focused on the touch of his finger, her skin aching for more contact. He pulls away, giving her a knowing look. Even as a human, he must know the hunger she feels, the need for touch. "No," she says, reaching out to grab his hand. She moves faster than she expects, and she ends up smacking herself in the face with his hand. "Oof," she says, dropping his hand and putting her own to her face.

"Yes," he says, smirking a little, his handsome face still charming despite the lack of supernatural appeal. "You're fast and strong now. It takes a little bit to get used to."

Amberleigh shakes her head, trying to focus around the barrage of new sensations.

"I don't need to get used to it," she reminds him. "This is only until Thursday night."

"Have fun," he encourages her, a hint of a smile curling his lips. "Live a little."

"What do you suggest?" she asks, suddenly entranced by the motion of his throat as he speaks, the faint line of the vein she can see on his neck, even in the darkness.

"Drink," he says immediately, "but somewhere private. Bring someone home and relish the experience. Then make them forget." Amberleigh knows that she can do that, her ability as a Holder allowing her to understand the new power she possesses. It will take a little bit to gain nuanced control, but she inherently knows the basics.

She nods, strong and confident in her new abilities. "What else?"

He cocks his head, considering. A soft shiver runs through him, and he hunches his shoulders, tugging his coat closed and putting his hands in his pockets. He curses in French. "I forgot how cold it can be!"

Amberleigh tugs her scarf free and puts it around his very human neck, tucking the ends inside as she buttons up his coat. "I expect this back," she reminds him, giving a soft peck on his cheek.

"So what happens if I kiss you again?" he asks, longing obvious in his eyes.

Amberleigh considers him. "Honestly?" she replies. "I think I'll probably fuck you right against this wall if you touch me again right now."

His face flushes and then his expression falls. "Oh," he says, crestfallen. "I just thought…"

She reaches out to touch his face, gently this time, but still lifting his chin with her superior strength. "Believe me," she tells him, "I want to. But it would defeat the purpose."

"Could you do it again?" he asks, curiosity overtaking his desire. "If I make you cum right now, and you give my power back to me, could we start all over again and you take my power again?"

Amberleigh shakes her head. "Not really. It doesn't work if it's all at the same time. I need a break in between to … regroup. So, if I gave you back this power, we would need to take a long break, probably a slow walk back to the apartment and a quiet evening, before I could take it back again."

"A quiet evening?" he echoes. "Why not enjoy ourselves with some noise?"

She chuckles, the sound throaty. "We could—but it would be normal succubus noise—and that's not why you're here tonight, Lucard."

After a moment of consideration, he nods, though she can sense his disappointment. "Thursday, though…"

"Thursday, I will have you all to myself all night long," she promises him. "And then

A Walk In The Park

some. My apartment is light-proof, so I fully expect a fun-filled day after our bargain is concluded."

He smiles, the human desire in him obvious. "Of course," he agrees. His eyes narrow as another question hits him. "What happens if you kiss another creature now—while you have my power?"

Amberleigh smiles. "Nothing," she tells him. "This is a one-at-a-time ability. I can't hold another power until I release this one." She doesn't mention that the only way she can retain multiple powers is if the creature dies.

Like Odo.

She doesn't think the vampire will appreciate the knowledge. He seems about to speak, but another shiver causes him to hunch his shoulders, and she laughs, her own skin cold but not a problem in her vampiric state.

"Go," she tells him. "Get inside somewhere warm. I'll meet you Thursday evening at the apartment." She smiles. "Have fun—but come back to me in one piece."

"Of course, little Holder," he promises and hurries away into the night. She watches him until he turns the corner at the end of the path back to the street, but she lingers in the underpass, taking stock of her new abilities.

She is strong and impervious to the cold, her body responding instantly to her desire to move. She takes a few steps back and forth beneath the overpass, gauging the way her

Discovered

body moves as a vampire. Awkward at first, she gains enough control after a few moments to move gracefully, and then she moves out from the darkness of the underpass, allowing her sensitive eyes time to adjust to the world she can now perceive. The park stands out in stark contrast of darks and lights, a hint of color bleeding into the lighter areas. She focuses on the space beneath a light pole far down the path, narrowing her gaze until she masters the range of her eyesight. She can see exquisite details if she looks long enough, but a hint of movement catches her attention, and she follows the trail of a squirrel as it scurries across the path and up a tree to where more warm bodies huddle inside a hole in the trunk.

Small creatures, her blood whispers, *not enough. Not now.*

Satisfied that she has grasped the range of her new physical abilities, she moves deeper into the park, determined to master her new desires before heading back into the streets where more tempting humans walk.

Chapter 3

This is the last time, I swear

Amberleigh has forgotten how strong the bloodlust can be, and the humans she passes on the street have started to degenerate into walking bags of blood by the time she is back in the neighborhood near the penthouse. She needs to find someone to bring home before her need grows stronger.

Breathe, she tells herself, trying to drown out the background noise of so many beating hearts, so much blood rushing through human veins, so much pleasure available if she would just reach out and grasp it. *Just breathe. Focus. Find a suitable partner for tonight. Someone who can stand to lose some energy—and some blood.*

Approaching the bar that used to be Rusty's, now called the Lion's Den, she sees the line of eager humans huddled out front, waiting to get inside to mingle with the supernatural creatures within. The humans don't know the truth of those they want to be closer to—but something pulls them back to this place night after night. She can find a creature inside who will serve her needs—but she has to get past the humans first—and that seems like a lot of unnecessary effort given the bloodlust swimming through her veins.

She has nearly convinced herself that it's not a terrible idea to feed on one of the humans waiting in line—that the human will *probably* survive the encounter. The wind gusts, bringing a waft of warm blood just waiting to be released, so she forces herself to turn the corner abruptly, ducking down the alley between the Lion's Den and the neighboring building. When she isn't Holding, Amberleigh uses this alley to dodge the blistering wind that whips down the avenue from the river, but her vampire skin is impervious to the weather tonight. Occasionally, she'll even spend an evening inside the Lion's Den, leaving with one of the supernatural creatures who frequent the bar, but it's been a little while since she was here.

I just need to find someone for the night, she reminds herself, trying to recall who may be inside right now. *Someone who can survive me right now.*

"Hey Leigh!"

She turns to the sound, her vampire eyes immediately locating the speaker. The tall

This Is The Last Time, I Swear

man leans casually against the side of the building down the alley, the back door next to him propped open by an old office chair. She recognizes the employee entrance to the Lion's Den, and her old friend, the bartender. The fact that he's an incubus makes him the answer to her dreams tonight.

"Tony," she breathes, speeding up to reach the demon.

Oh, fuck.

She remembers her face just in time.

Focusing for a moment, she retreats into herself, bypassing the borrowed vampire powers long enough to pull on one of her inherent abilities, subtly altering her appearance so she is the Leigh that her old friend will recognize up close. The change isn't drastic, just enough to make an acquaintance of Amberleigh's pause, that awkward, "Sorry, I thought you were someone else" that allows her to pass mostly unrecognized through the streets of the busiest city in the world. She settles into her Leigh face, adding the small tattoo on her hip that he will recall. She still wears the same black coat that he can recognize—probably a mistake if she really wants to keep her identities separate—but it pairs so well with her black dress and boots. None of that seems to matter though amid the pounding in her ears, the pulse of so many living creatures nearby.

Discovered

Using her shapeshifter ability always makes her remember the unfortunate circumstances that led to her keeping the power permanently, but it has definitely come in handy over the years, allowing her to keep three separate personas in the same area. Amberleigh works with vampires and werewolves—her face has bigger eyes and a rounder face—flushed, pink cheeks and a healthy glow. Leigh frequents the bars and deals with demons—her eyes narrow and her chin pointy—her body tight and limber. Amber treats with the fae—and always uses her true form because fae can sense deception—and while she knows shapeshifting is truth in a biological sense, others she encounters do not agree and would see it differently, calling her a liar if she changed her face. She is glad she doesn't have to resort to a fae tonight. Her head is too clouded to keep herself safe. Likely, she'd wake in the morning bound as a pet to some eccentric fairy.

Leigh heads past the connecting alley that leads back out to the street and the line of humans eager to get inside and take their chances. Tony would recognize her no matter what face she wears, knowing the taste of her magic, the pull of her distinct power, but still, it is better to be consistent. He doesn't know about her shifter ability. No one does.

The demon takes one final puff of his cigarette before putting it out, flicking the butt into the dumpster a few feet away. He shivers, only wearing a button-down shirt, sleeves partially rolled up, and shoves his hands into his pockets as he turns to face her again.

She narrows her eyes at him, nodding at the dumpster. "I thought you quit."

He shrugs. "I did." He lets out a sigh that encompasses an entire series of novels, then raises an eyebrow at her, shifting his attention from his own issues to hers. "I didn't think I'd see you around here tonight," he says, gesturing her closer. "Come in out of this wind!"

Leigh obeys, following him inside to the small back office and moving aside as he tugs the chair inside behind them. The door slams shut, the sound echoing inside Leigh's head, doubling over the sound of Tony's heartbeat. She watches his body as he moves, cataloging the broad shoulders she recalls, the narrow hips and long legs calling forth a more familiar desire. Tony makes sure the door is firmly shut, then standing up to face her, he narrows his eyes again, taking in her appearance, no doubt scanning her aura and feeling the difference. He probably can't sense the vampire power inside her, but he can tell she isn't all herself. "You Holding?"

She nods, transfixed by the line of his body visible through the white shirt, the veins tracing up his neck above the collar of his shirt. Even in the dimly lit back hallway-turned-office, her vampire eyes can see every detail.

Tony smirks, the grin highlighting the shape of his lips, and she wants to kiss those lips, badly. His eyes linger on her mouth, then meet her gaze again as he studies her face, watching her lips as well. Leigh runs her tongue along a new fang, the sensation sending a thrill through her middle. There's another long moment where their auras press against one another, testing boundaries. She has slept with Tony occasionally over the years, each taking and receiving the energy they need to sustain themselves. He seems to sense her need tonight—and he's a much better option than one of the humans in line outside.

"Vampire?" he guesses as she bites her lower lip, revealing the edge of a fang, and his voice is quiet despite the music she can hear echoing from inside the bar. "I thought you weren't doing that anymore."

"I'm not," she tells him. "This is the last time."

Tony makes a non-committal noise that shows just how much he believes that, and she reaches out to slap his upper arm. She is stronger than she should be, though, and her hand makes a loud crack against his skin. To her surprise, Tony doesn't move, absorbing her blow.

"What happened to you?" she asks, stepping closer to study him. "You're so strong!"

She pats his arm, gently this time. "Sorry, by the way. Still learning my strength."

Tony looks down at her arm, then shakes his head. "Long story, Leigh, and I don't think you're listening tonight." His hand reaches out and finds hers, and then he is pushing her back, crushing her until her legs collide with the edge of the desk behind them. Leigh is strong, but she lets herself be pushed, relishing the feeling of being dominated despite her newfound strength. "Let me give you what you need, baby."

Tony doesn't waste any time, leaning down to claim her mouth with a passionate kiss, his tongue ravishing her mouth with the promise of more satisfaction to come. Leigh returns the kiss just as forcefully, burying her hands in his dirty blonde hair, waiting a moment before she lets her mouth close a little bit, using her new teeth to nip his tongue just a little. The blood is a bright spark in her mouth, and her world narrows to the explosion of her senses. Colors whirl across the back of her eyelids and her body tenses in that familiar way just before the release of orgasm. She moans, and Tony pulls back just a little, releasing her mouth and licking his lips.

"Like that, is it?" he whispers, and she nods, unable to speak. He gives a quick glance around, and she manages to follow his gaze, noting the basic desk she leans against, the worn office chair on the far side, the few file cabinets against the wall, the tiny space they are shoved inside. "You need more?"

She nods her head, part of her disgusted by the idea of sex in the back room of the Lion's Den, but a stronger part of her not caring where they are. They certainly aren't the first ones to fuck back here. She needs two things—immediately: blood and sex. Normally, she wants sex more, but right now, the taste of his blood is still teasing her tongue, and she wants both right now.

"Not here," Tony says, breaking into her lust haze. She follows his gaze over her shoulder to the phone sitting on the desk.

"What?" she asks, her voice tinged with annoyance. "Why?"

"That is the only phone in this entire bar," he explains. He nods at the corner, and Leigh can see the outline of two bags. "And this is where the girls keep their shit when they're working. Anyone can come back here at any time."

The idea of being interrupted only excites her more, her desire cranking up another notch. Leigh reaches out, her hand tracing the buttons of Tony's shirt. When she reaches the final button, she grips it, jerking him hard against her. Her hand slips beneath the shirt, finding the edge of his jeans, and her deft fingers release the button of his jeans, dipping inside to grip him. She smirks up at him, pleased at the hard fullness against her palm. "Up for a challenge?" she teases.

"Always," Tony breathes heavily, then bends back down to kiss her again. His tongue still holds the trace of blood from her first nip, and she pulls him close with her free hand, clutching his neck. Tony's hands slide around her hips, then move up to shove the coat off her shoulders. Tugging it free, he tosses it aside, then lifts her a little, resting her on the edge of the desk. She opens her legs automatically, pulling him against her. Her dress strains against her thighs, her shawl sliding off one shoulder, and Tony quickly shoves her dress up, the material gathering at her waist. She releases her hold on his cock for a moment, just to adjust herself on the desk, while Tony drops to his knees, hands sliding along her tights up to her thighs. He tries to tug on the black material, pauses, then gives it a closer look.

"Oh fuck," she says, recalling that she is wearing the lined tights tonight. She hadn't planned on having sex like this—though now she realizes how foolish her planning has been. Of course, she would need to have sex with all this vampire power rushing through her.

Tony tugs at the material, curious. "Wait," he says, pulling a small area away from her skin. She shivers, the touch so close and yet still not what she needs. "These are the lined ones, right? I've seen these online!"

She chuckles, running her hands through his hair as she looks down at him.

"They look great," he comments, hands moving up slowly to where her thighs meet. "But I'm going to need to see some skin." He pauses, giving her a quizzical look. "How much do you love these?"

Leigh tries to follow his words, but it takes a moment for them to penetrate. "Oh," she says, considering. "I love them," she admits, "but I have more pairs at home."

Tony nods, face hovering just above just where she needs him. She puts her hands on the desk, ready to lift her butt and shimmy out of the tights, but then Tony grabs a small section of the black material between thumb and forefinger and yanks. The tights split with a small, soft rip and Tony reaches a hand around to slide her closer to his mouth, fingers widening the rip in the tights so he can access the skin he seeks. "There you are," he croons, then kisses her, soft lips gentle for that first caress.

Leigh grabs a fistful of hair in her hand and arches her back, moaning as he settles into a quick rhythm, one hand squeezing her ass while the other slides two fingers inside. She begins to cum almost immediately, pent-up desire releasing in a flood of magic, and part of her knows that if she doesn't rein it in, her power could swamp the entire bar, turning the place into a huge orgy. The image only excites her more, and she shudders against Tony's face, the first release taking the edge off her need. He looks up at her, gauging her response, and she gestures for him to stand up, curling her finger at him. He stands up, and she spins him around, pushing him so he sits down hard on the desk next to her. The old metal of the desk legs groans but holds firm. His pants are unbuttoned, and she leans over, lifting his shirt out of the way so she can take his length in her mouth.

"Leigh," he moans as she sucks deep, relishing the feel of his hardness in her mouth. One hand slides down to cup his balls while the other strokes him in time with her mouth. The benefit of Tony is that she can make him cum with her mouth and he will still be ready to fuck right after–unlike human men who need time to get hard again. She takes her time, enjoying the sounds he makes as she sucks his cock, soaking up the tendrils of his power with her succubus ability, but also logging the small details of his body with her new senses–the way his heart rate stutters when she sucks hard, the soft sheen of sweat on his upper lip, the erect hairs on his forearms as he wraps his hands in her hair and sets a rhythm. She lets herself be moved as he likes, relishing the build of his desire. When he is close, she drags her newly sharpened fangs lightly across his shaft, her bite gentle enough to disappear beneath the pleasure, and she drinks

Discovered

greedily of both his blood and his cum when he explodes. She leaves him in her mouth for a few moments after, looking up his body to watch his chest shudder a few times. She can hear his pounding heart slowing down. Letting him go with an audible pop, she leans up, about to speak, when the door to the office flies open.

"Seriously, Tony? Ew." A petite, dark-haired woman stands in the doorway, her tone clearly disapproving. Leigh turns her head away from the door, hovering over Tony's crotch, her back to the vampire at the door. "I thought you went home."

Tony, completely unfazed to be discovered sprawled on the desk with his cock hanging out, chuckles, then crooks his neck, giving Leigh a small smile. "I was just leaving," he tells his co-worker. He pulls his pants closed with one hand and offers the other to Leigh, who gets to her feet with her back still to the woman at the door. She tugs her dress back down, then ducks to retrieve her shawl from the floor, trying to straighten her appearance without letting the vampire see her face. She knows the vampire can sense that she is a succubus, but she may not feel Lucard's power—she doesn't know Leigh the way Tony does. Right now, being seen as a quick hookup in the back room seems the best solution. Leigh knows Tony—and she knows that he works with two vampire bartenders—but she'd prefer the vampire not know who she is right now.

Tony plucks her coat from the desk and wraps it around her, keeping her facing him. He lifts the hood over her head, tucking her blonde hair inside, then winks at her as he buttons her coat up from the bottom. When she is covered, he steps away from her to a file cabinet, opens the bottom drawer, and pulls out a leather jacket. Shrugging into his coat, he pushes Leigh before him to the back door. They exit into the alley, the cold wind immediately whooshing up Leigh's dress and finding her newly exposed skin through the ripped tights.

She lets out a muffled yelp at the sensation. The cold doesn't bother her as a vampire, but with her newfound senses, the feeling is startling. She reaches out to grab Tony's hand, already anticipating the long night ahead.

"I assume your place," he says when they leave the alley for the main street. "I have lots of windows." In the past, they have hooked up in back rooms and empty rooms at parties, but she has never brought him back to her places in the city. Once, they stumbled back to her place in Brooklyn, but Tony isn't a client — he's a friend.

Leigh nods, leading him down the sidewalk at a fast walk. "So does mine," she replies, "but they all close tight at sunrise." Tony hasn't been to her penthouse, but she doesn't think she can last the long ride to Brooklyn tonight. For a moment, she considers taking him to her walk-up, but common sense overrides the lust hazing her brain. Tony is a friend—a convenient hook-up who understands her needs—but he isn't someone she wants to take back to the only place she truly views as home. That space is for her. The penthouse will be fine. Tony knows she is wealthy.

"We better hurry then," he teases, keeping pace with her easily. "I want to be inside when everything locks down."

"You will be," Leigh promises. "Deep inside."

Chapter 4

Old friends in new positions

Leigh's common sense has somewhat returned by the time they reach her building, and she gives a quick glance around as they walk inside, using her vampire senses to locate the people around them. The doorman doesn't seem concerned as they enter the lobby, giving her expensive coat one glance before returning his attention to the screen in front of him. Leigh can hear the low hum of the announcer echoing from the earbud in his ear–the hockey game is in overtime with one minute left until they resort to the shootout. She retrieves her keycard from the clutch jammed in her pocket, calling the elevator.

No one else is in the lobby, and Leigh allows herself to relax. This is Amberleigh's penthouse, after all. Bringing Tony here as

Discovered

Leigh is risky, especially if one of the vampires in the city passes by. Listening to the heartbeat of the incubus holding her hand, Leigh finds it hard to care. After what seems like an extraordinarily long wait—the overtime is over and they are setting up for the shootout—the elevator arrives with a bright ding. Leigh drags Tony inside, not waiting for the door to close completely before she tugs him close, claiming his mouth with a passionate kiss. Tony doesn't waste any time, pressing her back against the shiny silver wall. She hooks a leg up around his hip, annoyed when her coat restricts her movement. Without missing a beat, Tony has her buttons undone, and his hand is sliding up her thigh to cup her ass beneath the dress. They kiss for a long moment, but when Leigh pauses to catch her breath, she realizes that the elevator isn't moving.

"Shit," she breathes, kicking her foot out to press the long button with the words "Penthouse" on it at the top of the wall of numbered buttons. The elevator dings, prompting her to flash her keycard for access, and she grunts, spinning both of them so she can whisk the card over the sensor without letting go of the incubus in her arms. Tony chuckles as they move, then bends to kiss her neck as the elevator finally starts to rise. Leigh glances up, watching the numbers on the display count up—5, 10, 15—Tony's hands slide up her back beneath the dress, eliciting a shiver—20, 25,

30—his mouth finds the sweet spot where her shoulder meets her neck, and she melts into him—35, 36, 37. The last three floors slide by too slowly, and when the doors finally slide open on the 40th floor, she spins him out of the elevator, pushes him down the short hallway to her front door, then fumbles with her clutch again to find her keys as Tony presses himself behind her, hands cupping her breasts as he continues to kiss her neck.

Leigh curses herself as she searches for the key, a small, still coherent, part of her mind knowing that the separation from the public elevator to her private doorway is significant, that it allows her to invite specific vampires inside, but right now, the key is a detriment, slowing her down and blocking her from getting what she wants—Tony naked and inside her, now.

She finally gets the key in the lock, twisting it quickly, glad that she rarely locks the top lock. When she got her first shoebox apartment on the Lower East Side, she would alternate which lock she engaged, thinking that any would-be criminal would assume both were locked and pick both, thereby unlocking one as they engaged the other. She's not sure if her theory is practical, but no one ever broke into her apartment—even when she lived in sketchy neighborhoods back in the beginning.

She hasn't thought of that small space in years, and as Tony presses against her and the door unlocks, the two of them falling into the hallway in a tangle of limbs, she is glad that she can now afford nice things.

Risk equals reward, she thinks, her father's voice echoing in her head, and the sound nearly kills her mood. She pushes any fatherly advice away, focusing on the eager man currently tugging her coat down her arms, abandoning it on the hallway floor as they move into the apartment. He spins her around, using the shawl still wrapped around her shoulders to swing her so her back faces him, and the front of her thighs hit the back of the couch in the living room. Tony pushes her forward, leaning her over the furniture as he yanks her dress up around her waist. Without a word, his strong hands grip her tights, and she feels the rip as he tears them from the waistband down to the hole he made earlier. She hears him unzip his pants, and then he is pressed between her legs, hard length teasing with promise.

"You want me?" he growls, one hand gripping her hip, and the other grabbing her shoulder and tugging her up with the shawl, so he can kiss the back of her neck.

"Fuck yes!" she demands, lifting a knee onto the couch to give him better access. She isn't very tall, and Tony's long legs put his cock just slightly too high for her if her feet stay on the floor. She pushes against him, arching her back to give her the angle she craves, and then he slides inside. She groans with satisfaction, her vampire senses transforming a normally delightful sensation into something exquisite. The feeling builds instantly, and then she is crying out, pushing back into him, demanding more—she knows he can take it. Tony increases his pace, fucking her hard the way he knows she wants, and soon she is shuddering on his cock, the orgasm a kaleidoscope of exploding colors behind her eyelids. She hovers in that space for a long moment, relishing the feeling with her borrowed vampire powers.

When she comes down from that first high, she glances over her shoulder to see Tony smirking down at her, still hard and eager, but pausing to give her time to collect herself.

"You are so damn sexy," he moans, hand tightening on her hip as he pulls her back onto his cock, the motion slow this time, teasing. She bites her lip, her fangs drawing blood, and her tongue darts out to lick it. "Vixen," he murmurs, his other hand reaching up to rest on her shoulder as he settles into a steady slow pace. "Tell me what you want."

"That," she moans, pushing back into each thrust. "Just fuck me like that." One of the best things about Tony is his ability to follow instructions—he continues to slide slowly in and out, keeping a steady rhythm for a time before picking up on her need for more.

"More?" he asks, and when she presses back enthusiastically, he obliges, increasing both speed and pressure, and soon he is pushing her over the edge again. This time, she is more prepared for the daze that follows and takes a moment to lift her other leg up on the couch so she can slide limply over to land on the cushions. She doesn't need to catch her breath, the vampire powers allowing her to recover immediately, but her mind still reels from the overwhelming sensations. Tony walks around the couch, then pauses to kneel near where she slumps into a languid pile. His hand is gentle as he first touches her calf, tugging her foot close so he can unzip her boot. He tosses the boot across the room to land against the wall near the front door, soon joined by her other boot. Then his hands pull her legs until they are straight on the couch. He slides the remains of the tights down, balling them up and tossing them aside. Leigh watches him with dazed eyes, fascinated by the city lights reflecting through the window on his face, coloring his hair in shades of white and silver.

Still touching her gently, he moves her so she sits up, locating the bottom of her dress and tugging it over her head. It joins the pile of her tights somewhere across the room. She sits very still, now wearing only her bra, which he unhooks easily, twirling it on one finger for a moment with a crooked grin before letting it fly away across the room. Leigh snorts at the sight.

"Seriously? You are like a twelve-year old boy with a toy," she teases, stretching out on the couch, enjoying his eyes on her bare skin.

He raises an eyebrow, then reaches up to tug off his shirt the way she always loves, gripping it behind his neck and pulling it forward over his head, revealing the gorgeous body she recalls. He wriggles his hips, his jeans sliding down as he shuffles forward on his knees, hard cock prominently displayed. He sees her eyes watching him, then grins. "If anyone is delighted with a new toy," he says, moving forward to tug her legs so she faces him, her back against the couch cushions, "I'd say you're pretty fascinated by what you brought home tonight."

"More like an old favorite toy," she says, then reaches out to grab his cock, hands stroking him several times as he moves her closer, sliding her butt slightly off the edge of the couch so he can get the angle right. She lines up his cock, feeling the tip press inside, then slides her hand over her clit, rubbing slightly as she squeezes the cock tip inside. Tony's hand covers hers, rubbing her clit as he slips inside a little more. "Oh, did I neglect you?" he croons, leaning down to suck her nipple. "You need more attention?" Leigh lets her head fall back, her hand giving way to his experienced fingers, which begin to rub her in time with his slow even thrusts.

"Oh yes," she moans, feeling the orgasm quickly spiral up from her middle, her body clenching tightly as he makes her cum again. Her succubus power swirls, pulling energy from Tony, who pulls it back just as easily, each feeding and renewing the other with pleasure.

As her succubus power begins to wane, Leigh becomes aware of the vampire she Holds, and she sits up slowly, then moves Tony's hand away from her clit and up to her breast. She rocks forward, still keeping his cock inside her, and he sits back on his heels as she moves to the floor, wrapping her legs around his hips and holding him tight. She reaches up and grips his hair, twisting hard and making him look at her.

"I want to bite you," she tells him, enjoying the lust in his eyes at the words. "Can I taste you?"

"Hell yeah," Tony whispers hoarsely, moving his head to expose his neck. "Drink while you fuck me, baby. Ride me while you bite me."

Leigh leans down, her mouth first kissing the side of his neck, one hand still buried in his hair while the other splays against his back. She rocks her hips faster, setting a hard rhythm against him, soaking in the pleasure before she opens her mouth and bites with her new fangs.

The blood fills her mouth, rich and sensual, and she drinks deeply, her body alight with joy. Tony grunts, trying to fuck her harder, but can't with her on top setting the rhythm. He groans, then stands up, lifting her easily — Leigh makes a mental note to ask him about his newfound strength at some point — and takes the few steps to the large window. He presses her against it, the glass cold against her back, but she doesn't let go of his neck, mouth working fiercely to explore this new form of pleasure.

"Fucking hell," he moans, driving into her with wild abandon now, lost to his own pleasure as he seeks his own release. "You are amazing!" he shouts, and Leigh feels the power of his orgasm as it floods both of them. When Leigh comes to her senses, they are crumpled on the floor, Tony gasping as he catches his breath, his cock sliding out of her as he reaches up to touch the bite mark on his neck.

Leigh frowns at the red half-circle she left behind, her bite crude from her eagerness. "I think I can heal it," she says, "if you want."

Tony chuckles, studying the red on his fingers as he pulls his hand away. "Nah, I like it." He sits up, leaning against the bottom of the window. "War wounds," he comments, grinning at her.

Leigh smiles, body settling as satisfaction rolls over her. "Glad you survived the battle," she comments.

"Oh yeah," Tony says, "and I'm looking forward to the next skirmish." At her expression, he laughs, then raises an eyebrow. "A break first, I think, though." He glances around the apartment, taking in the big screen TV across from the couch. "Netflix?" he asks teasingly.

"We already started the chill part," Leigh says, "but we can watch until something else comes up." Her gaze catches the mark on the glass window, a clear imprint of her ass, and she smirks.

Tony follows the line of her sight, then frowns. "You have a cleaning service?"

Leigh shakes her head. "Nothing some Windex won't fix." She gives him a mischievous grin. "How many marks you think we can get on there by morning?"

Tony smirks. "Challenge accepted."

Chapter 5

Big brothers don't care how old you are

The blaring ringtone drags Amber from the sleep of the dead, and she groans loudly, arms reaching blindly for the source of the sound. Her hand flails, hitting the phone on her nightstand, and she fumbles with it, trying to silence the noise. Failing to stop the sound of Michael Jackson singing about Billie Jean, she cracks open an eye, vampiric sight allowing her to see even in the darkness. Angrily, she jams the red button to deny the call, in no mood to talk to her brother even at the best of times, never mind when she's high on vampire powers and humming with sexual satisfaction.

Discovered

"Amby," Benjamin Miller demands, his voice echoing in the shuttered room, "why did it take you so long to answer?"

Amber groans, squinting to stare at the phone. *Fuck, I hit the wrong button.*

"Are you still in bed?" her big brother asks, judgment clear in his tone. "What's going on? Are you sick?"

Her brother's questions awaken her immediately, and she stares at the phone, seeing Ben's face filling the screen. *Oh fuck.* She glances quickly to her left, where Tony had been when they collapsed into her bed around noon. The satin sheets are rumpled, but the bed is empty. *Thank fucking god for small favors.* Tony was always good about not overstaying his welcome.

"No," she manages, tilting the phone so he can only see the ceiling and the slowly rotating fan. "I took a nap." She glances down at her naked body, finds the sheet balled at the foot of the bed, and tugs it up over herself, then runs a hand through her hair, attempting to smooth what must be obviously "just been fucked" hair. She takes a moment to fix her face, restoring the Amber her brother knows as she asks, "What time is it?"

"It's 5," he tells her suspiciously. "Why are you napping? Are you not sleeping well?"

Amber sniffs, her thoughts ordering themselves as she prepares a defense against her brother's demanding influence. "I'm fine,

Ben," she assures him, tilting the phone so it shows his face, her own frown visible from the bottom corner of the screen. "What's up? Is something wrong?"

"Do I need a reason to call my baby sister?" he asks, slight hurt in the question that Amber's vampire powers pick up on. She wonders if she would have noticed if she wasn't Holding.

"I guess not," she says, ignoring the stab of guilt. *Damn vampire sensitivity. For all the perks of this power, there are too many drawbacks.* After an awkward pause, she asks, "How are you?"

"Merry Christmas to you, too," he snaps, not satisfied by her tone. "And here I thought we should get together."

"You want to get together?" she echoes. "W–" She stops herself before the word *Why?* leaves her mouth, saying instead, "When?"

"How about now?" he asks. "You don't seem busy right now. Get cleaned up and meet me at Rusty's. Wait, it has a new name now... the something den?"

"No," she blurts, not wanting to run into either of the vampire bartenders who saw her in the back room with Tony yesterday. "Not there."

"Why not?" he asks. "We used to go there all the time."

"It's different now," she offers, not entirely lying, "with the new owners. It has a different vibe." She pauses, running through the options. *Ben wants to meet in a bar on Christmas Eve*, she thinks. *Where should we go?* "How about Mystic Apple?" She hasn't been to that upscale establishment in several months. No one will recognize her there.

"I guess so," he agrees, "but it's farther from your apartment. You don't mind, even in this weather?"

"Weather?" she echoes, recalling how little the cold had affected her. *Fuck, daylight*. She glances at the time on the phone screen, allowing Ben to catch sight of her face for a brief second. 5:17pm. *Good, it's already dark outside*.

"The snow?" he asks. "Seriously, Amby, you okay?"

"Oh!" she says, reaching over to find the remote that controls the darkened windows in her apartment. She sits up, tugging the sheet tight over her body, then hits the button to raise the light dampeners, wincing as the slightly brighter light from the skyline hits her sensitive eyes. "I'm fine," she assures her brother. "Just out of it from my nap." She pauses, then adds, "I just needed to use the sleep."

Ben chuckles, recalling their phrase for a hard nap during their college years, started after a particular nap on their parent's couch that had Ben waking up with drool on his face. When she asked if he was okay, he had said yes, but he just needed to use something... to use the sleeping ... then promptly rolled over and went back to sleep. It has been their joke for serious naps ever since. "I get it. How's work treating you these days?"

"Busy," she says, letting the sigh creep into her voice. Ben thinks she's a therapist, but since she insists that she sees people at home instead of an office, she wonders if he thinks she's an expensive call girl.

"Lots of people with problems?" he prompts, voice neutral. He always pushes a little bit, trying to catch her in a lie.

"Oh yeah," she agrees. "And I can only help so many people, you know?"

"Any interesting cases?"

She sighs, running her free hand through her hair. "Always—my latest is a guy who can't forget the life he had before, constantly longing for what he doesn't have anymore. You know the type?"

Ben snorts, buying her semi-truthful example. "I work with some of them. They love the money and the lifestyle but hate the dishonesty and pretense."

"Exactly!" she says. "How about you? Work still the same old?"

"You know how it is," he says. Amber doesn't let the frown show on her face. She doesn't know how it is—because Ben rarely tells her anything real about his life these days. "Chasing after people, checking up on reputations, forging alliances, the usual."

Discovered

"Sounds exciting," she comments. "You don't have anywhere to be today? No hot date tonight?"

"It's Christmas Eve, Amby," he reminds her. "Tonight is about family." He pauses, no doubt thinking of their dead parents, how she is the only family he has left now. "Why?" he adds after a moment. "Do you have a date tonight?"

"Yes," she says, inventing a reason to get away from Ben after a little bit of family time. "But not until later tonight."

"How late?" he asks, his voice shifting into Big Brother mode.

"Later," she repeats vaguely, not appreciating his tone.

"Amby, no one respectable meets late on Christmas Eve. Is he sneaking out on his family to see you?"

"Ben!" she exclaims, her annoyance with him boiling over. She can feel the last of her high from the mind-blowing sex and the satisfying blood evaporating from the room around her. "No, he's fucking not. I wouldn't date a married man anyway. Too many sexy single men to bother with that trouble."

"Please don't talk to me about sexy men," he groans.

"Then don't lecture me about my love life," she retorts.

"Fine," he agrees. "But we can still grab a quick dinner at the bar. Meet you there in an hour?"

Big Brothers Don't Care How Old You Are

Amber sniffs, calculating the time. She definitely needs a shower. She can't go see her brother smelling like the all-night sex marathon she just had, not to mention the streaks of dried blood she can feel on her body. She's glad the light from the phone screen isn't enough to show what she really looks like. She wonders how much her brother will notice her vampiric traits. Tony saw right away, but he is supernatural. Ben Miller is as normal as they come. *Besides,* she assures herself, *Mystic Apple has low lighting. He won't notice anything.*

"Fine," she agrees, "but I didn't get you anything."

"I would expect nothing less," he says with a laugh. "See you there, sis."

Amber snaps the phone shut, then sits for a moment, gathering herself before moving, feeling the vampire power within. She's still powerful, but she's more accustomed to it now. She can probably pull it deep inside, hide her borrowed nature for a few hours with her brother until she needs to drink again later tonight.

She stretches her legs out before her in the bed, vampire eyes studying her skin, taking stock of her body. She is sated, so blood shouldn't be a problem. She can be around people without too much temptation.

Yeah, she decides, *shower first, then coffee.* Thoughts of caffeine swirling in her brain, she rolls out of bed.

Chapter 6

It's not official if you eat at the bar

Mystic Apple is the same place Amber recalls, the long bar against the back wall opposite the sea of small tables, the mirrored wall nearly obscured by rows of high-end liquor bottles. She spies Ben immediately, her brother's broad shoulders encased in a tailored suit jacket, his blonde hair elegantly styled, a small tumbler of amber liquid at his side.

A tall brunette in a red dress leans against the bar next to him, her body language suggesting her willingness to move closer. Amber snorts, sensing the woman's desire from the door. The bar is filled with a blend of lust and desperation, and she pushes her succubus abilities down, not wanting to indulge while still Holding for the vampire. In the absence of her power, her vampire abilities swirl, and she can hear every heartbeat in the place, so much human desire pounding away through their veins. *Steady*, she reminds herself, pulling back on her senses and regaining her control. Just eat some dinner, talk a little bit, and head back home to get ready to find a suitable partner for tonight. *Maybe a shifter,* she thinks. *They are full of energy—and less picky about blood.*

She glances at her clothes, comfortable brown boots over tan leggings disappearing beneath a long white sweater and a respectable winter coat. The sweater has a high neck, just in case Ben decides to study her skin. Tony left a few marks–they will be gone by the evening, but she doesn't want to deal with any questions in the meantime. She gives her coat to the host, gesturing to Ben at the bar, and makes her way to the stool at his side. The brunette gives her a dark look as she settles in on Ben's far side, and Amber smiles at her, politely dismissive.

"Amber!" Ben exclaims, seeing her appear at his side. He gestures to the brunette. "This is Serina. She was just telling me how her date is an hour late. Can you believe that?"

"I cannot," Amber says, shaking her head. "How rude!"

"I know!" Ben says, then gives the woman a charming smile. "Tell you what—I'm going to have some dinner with my sister here. If

Discovered

your date doesn't show by the time we're done, how about you spend some time with me instead?"

The woman nods, her challenging attitude disappearing at the word sister, and slinks her way down the bar to an empty seat. The after-work crowd isn't overwhelming, but the bar is filling up quickly. The bartender makes his way over to stand in front of them. "Menu?" he asks.

"Yes please," Amber tells him, taking the small sheet of paper he hands her. She skims the offerings, seeing the truncated Christmas Eve options. The vampire in her rallies at the sight of the steak, and she nods, handing the paper back to the bartender. "Steak, please," she orders. "Rare."

The bartender gives her brother a look. "Same thing, huh?"

"It's family thing," Ben jokes. "You want the baked potato too?" The potato doesn't appeal as much as the steak, but Amber nods.

"All the way?" the bartender asks, and Amber senses the rush of annoyance from her brother as she smiles at the man. He is handsome, after all, and she loves a man in a bowtie. She likes to untie them and use the ends to guide the man's head where she wants it. Considering the dark hair, chiseled features, and knowing look in the bartender's eye, Amber knows he would be a good time—a one-night stand, of course. She would

It's Not Official If You Eat At The Bar

kill him if she tried more than that—but he would be a fun evening. Maybe next time when she isn't Holding. He won't survive both of her powers right now.

"Always," she tells him, enjoying the sense of frustration wafting from her brother.

"Good choice," the bartender tells her. Then he catches sight of Ben's face, and straightens up, flirtatious manner fading into professionalism. "Something to drink?"

"Sparkling water," she orders. "Pelegrino?"

"Done," he says, reaching under the bar to pour her a glass. He is brave enough to touch her fingers briefly as he slides the glass her way, then he is off down the bar, putting in their order and helping other customers.

"Seriously, Amby?" Ben asks.

"What?" she replies. "What did I do?"

Ben rolls his eyes, taking a sip of his drink. "You know what I mean. You can do better."

"Says the guy chatting up a stranger when I walked in?" she points out.

"She was lonely," Ben defends. "That's different."

"What you're really saying is that it's okay for you because you're a man, and it's not okay for me because I'm a woman. I can't believe you still cling to such outdated standards." She shakes her head at him.

"Don't try to psychoanalyze me," he says. "I'm not one of your clients."

Discovered

"Obviously," she snaps. "You'd be a better person if you were."

They sit in awkward silence for a moment, but when the bartender tries to catch her eye, Amber ignores him, not wanting to provoke her brother further. He won't work out tonight anyway.

"So," she says finally, trying to save the moment. "How's life?"

"Fine," Ben snaps. He shakes his head, then looks over at her, apology in his eyes. "I'm sorry, Amby. I just… I just want more for you. That's all."

"I know," she tells him. "I get it." She pauses, then asks, "Why do you still call me Amby?"

"Because you'll always be my baby sister," he says, giving her a soft bump with his shoulder, "no matter how old you are."

"That's how time works," she ribs him. "You'll always be my big brother." She snorts, then adds, "But I stopped calling you Benji years ago."

"Mom and dad never stopped," he says quickly, tipping the glass onto an edge and rolling it on the bar top, the liquid inside sloshing slowly around in circles. "I was the only 25-year-old Benji in the world."

"Yeah," Amber agrees. "Even the dog didn't live that long."

"Jerk," Ben says, elbowing her in the side. He smiles, though. "You know it's only because I care about you, right?"

It's Not Official If You Eat At The Bar

Amber sighs, deflating a bit. "I know." She gives him a serious look. "What is it you want me to do, Ben? What am I not doing that you want me to do?"

"I don't even know anymore," he admits. "I don't know anything about your life these days."

"Well, it's fine," she assures him. "Work is constant. Money is good. The apartment is awesome."

"I can't believe you still live in that tiny walk-up," he comments, and Amber takes a sip of her water, realizing how close she came to mentioning the penthouse. Ben doesn't know about her other houses. He thinks she still lives in her first apartment after college. She does—just not when she's working.

"It's cozy," she defends, thinking of the small one-bedroom apartment with its tiny refrigerator, so different from the penthouse she left an hour ago.

"But don't you want more? I mean, are you lonely?"

"Hardly," she scoffs. "I'm rarely alone, Ben. Remember my date tonight?"

He shakes his head. "I'm not talking about that. I mean something real." He pauses, then an idea seems to strike him. "What about Celia?" he asks. "Have you seen her lately?"

Amber raises an eyebrow at him. "What makes you bring her up?"

"Just curious," he says. "You used to see her all the time. How long has it been?"

"Actually, she just called asking me to get together on New Year's," Amber tells him. "She's got a new beau, in case that's what you are angling for."

He scoffs. "Celia is lovely, but not for me," he says. "She wants you to go out with them on New Year's? You should."

"Yeah," Amber says, dismissively. She has no idea how she will be feeling a week from now—if the vampire power will affect her the way Gerard did so many years ago. She doesn't think so, but she also doesn't want to make promises she can't keep.

"It's easy to get lost," Ben warns, his voice ominous. "We get so caught up in our lives that we forget that the people are what make them worth living."

Amber doesn't reply, simply stares at her big brother, wondering what has prompted his soul-searching. A feeling wafts from him— deep loneliness—and she tries to pull away, not wanting to know such things about her brother. When the bartender appears with two plates and sets them on the bar top, Amber is relieved for the distraction. She doesn't want to face her brother's demons. Not tonight when she is high on vampire powers.

"I haven't forgotten you, Ben," she says quietly, reaching for the steak knife. The small puddle of red juice beneath the steak calls to

It's Not Official If You Eat At The Bar

her, and she digs into the red meat, savoring the tease of almost-blood on her tongue. She grabs her water, taking a drink to wash the meat down, and finds Ben staring at her.

"Hungry?" he asks, eyebrows raised.

Amber ducks her head, wiping her mouth with the napkin. "What of it? I'm not allowed to enjoy a good steak now?"

"That's not enjoying a steak, Amby," he says, his voice teasing big brother again. "That's inhaling a chunk of red meat like you haven't eaten in days."

She elbows him, glass in hand, and is alarmed when he rocks on the stool. *Fuck*, she reminds herself, *my strength*. Ben catches himself, giving her a horrified look. "Been working out?" he asks.

"Mmm-hmm." She nods, cutting a second, smaller piece of meat and chewing it politely like the sister he knows. He watches her for another moment, then satisfied with her normal human eating habits, he turns to his own steak. They sit quietly for a few minutes, enjoying the meal and the hum of the bar around them. Amber has moved on to take random bites of the potato between her steak, stretching out the flavor, when a hand lands on her shoulder. At the same time, she smells blood—and not the weak version from her plate. Someone in the bar is bleeding—profusely. She shrugs the hand off her body

Discovered

automatically, spinning quickly to see who has touched her.

The human standing before her is struggling to stand, his heart pounding hard to keep him upright despite the lack of blood inside his veins.

Oh, fuck.

Chapter 7

A quick refresher on bathroom etiquette

Lucard stands behind her stool, weaving drunkenly, his eyes too wide and puffy for his human face. "Wha–?" she hears Ben ask, turning to see who has disturbed his sister, and Amber hops off the stool, very aware that she is not wearing the proper face. If Lucard weren't fighting so hard to stay upright, he probably would have noticed the subtle changes. Maybe he notices, but he is too far gone to say something.

He didn't find me, Amber realizes. *He found his power. He tracked it here.*

Fuck.

She scans the human before her, trying to gauge the situation with her vampire senses, and the strong scent of blood smothers her.

He's bleeding badly—both inside and out. She looks over his dark coat, glad that his clothing is covering the damage.

"I..." Lucard slurs, and she can see that some of his teeth are broken when he opens his mouth. "I need..."

"Who is this?" Ben demands.

"A friend," she says, walking the wobbly Lucard away from the bar and her brother. "I'll just see to him. Be right back!" She calls the last cheerily, then disappears into the milling crowd that has filled the bar since they arrived.

"What are you doing here?" she hisses in Lucard's ear. "We're not supposed to meet until Thursday! What the hell happened to you?"

"Need ... back," he slurs, nearly walking into the back of a man in a gray suit. Amber catches him in time, handling his weight easily with his vampire strength.

Okay, she thinks, assessing her options quickly. *He's hurt—and he needs his vampire power back to heal properly, or this can end very badly.* She glances around, looking between the heads of the people in the bar. *I need somewhere private to take him.*

For the first time, she is sorry that her power doesn't simply allow her to return his abilities to him. It doesn't work that way, no matter how much she wishes it did right now. The only way to return his power is for him to make her cum—a daunting prospect at the moment.

And where can I take him? I'm totally not dressed for any of this. An idea hits her, and she groans, but doesn't waste more time trying to think of something else. She can smell the blood on him, in him, and it's growing stronger. Lucard the human doesn't have much time left.

Fine. She heaves a huge sigh, trying not to let the refrain of "Told you this was a bad idea to mess with vampires again" echo in her mind as she herds Lucard toward the bathroom doors. She pauses before the two doors, debating the odds of being disturbed. With another long-suffering sigh, she heads for the men's room, knowing that they are less likely to draw attention in the stall there. Mystic Apple may be an upscale establishment, but people always fuck in bathrooms.

Amber hasn't fucked in a bathroom stall since college, but she remembers how it's done. Pushing the door open and holding Lucard in front of her, she is relieved to see that the room is empty for the moment. She doesn't pause, moving to the farthest stall from the door, then pushes him inside, letting him collapse to sit on the toilet. He doesn't even seem to notice their surroundings, another sign of how far gone he is. The vampire she met the night before would never find himself in such a place.

Discovered

At least it's clean.

She shuts and locks the stall door behind her, then stands for a moment, trying to work out how to have an orgasm from a half-dead human slumping to the side. This feels all kinds of wrong—and not just because she's in a bathroom stall.

"Fuck it," she says, grabbing Lucard's hand and jamming it down her pants. Lucard moans in pain, glancing up as his fingers touch her bare skin, and she notices the awkward angle of his wrist, the joint twisted too far for a normal human wrist to bend.

"Seriously?" she groans, feeling slightly guilty as she tries to gently remove his damaged hand from her pants, but he resists, pressing his dislocated wrist awkwardly against her skin as her succubus power works to rouse him despite his injuries. If men are anything, it is predictable. She can see him trying to focus, but he's also severely wounded. She's going to have to help him along. She abandons the wounded hand, knowing he'll figure it out, and leans down, fingers unbuttoning his coat, vampire senses scenting the blood before she sees it, but it is still a lot— more than a human can survive losing.

"Lucard," she says, pity filling her at the sight of the gouges in his dark shirt. She pushes the coat back and off his shoulders where it bunches at his elbows. For a moment, she worries that the vampire in her will

A Quick Refresher On Bathroom Etiquette

demand the blood, but Lucard's power seems to sense its owner, and the stickiness coating him holds no appeal for her.

Sensible of her exit strategy, she tugs the white sweater over her head and hooks it on the bathroom door behind her, not wanting to get blood on it. Her coat is at the coat check, and she won't have any cool vampire abilities to make people not notice her as she leaves the bar. The cool air in the bathroom caresses her bare skin, and she shivers slightly, her nipples hardening beneath the basic t-shirt bra she wears under her tank top. After a second glance at the blood coating Lucard, she pauses, shrugging the cream tank top off as well and stowing it behind her. No reason to walk home in a wet tank top, after all, and the blood would never come out all the way. Wearing only her bra, leggings, and boots, she scoots closer on his lap, her hands moving his legs so he provides a steady base beneath her. Her hand brushes his cock, a small bulge that has started to fade after her initial push of succubus power. Lucard is dying.

"No, you don't," she tells him, grabbing him by the hair and tugging his head close to her for a hard kiss. His mouth moves, pressing against hers as her power pulls his life force to the surface again, and the bulge beneath her grows into something more impressive. Her hands work at his chest, tugging the buttons free, trying to touch him where he isn't wounded. She moves to his neck, kissing in the way she knows will rouse him, and her eyes glance down at the chest she has revealed. He wears the tattered remains of an undershirt, but no corset, and lines crisscross the chest beneath, deep claw marks into his skin. She grips the neckline with one hand and gives a quick tug, ripping the fabric easily, then reaches down to squeeze one of his exposed nipples.

Lucard moans, rallying from the sensation of her hands on him.

"Did you mess with a shifter?" she breathes, her other hand darting down to caress his cock through the pants. "Foolish boy—what were you thinking?"

"Not ... a ... boy," he manages, and she looks up to meet his suddenly alert gaze, echoes of the vampire she had met the night before showing through the pain.

"I hope not," she tells him. "You need to make me cum if you want your power back," she reminds him. "I can't do it alone."

"Wouldn't ... dream ... of it," he manages, moving a hand between their bodies, clearly intending to put it down her pants. He winces, then looks down, noting the odd angle of his wrist, prominent now. "Oh," he says, then looks up at her. He seems to notice something, the pain bringing him sharply around, and he peers at her face. "Amberleigh?" he asks,

A Quick Refresher On Bathroom Etiquette

an eyebrow raised as he studies her eyes, the shape of her nose.

Amber nods, waiting for him to explain his confusion, then she remembers her face. *I'm a fucking idiot.* She looks away, letting her hair fall over her face, and busies herself with his pants. If he can't help her with his hands, she's going to have to do this another way.

Slowly, she begins altering her appearance, shifting a tiny element at a time, while her hands work at his waist, easily unzipping his pants and tugging free an impressive cock. "Damn," she moans, nipples tightening at the thought of what the vampire could do with that if he weren't injured right now. She has finished altering her eyes and nose, working on her mouth and jawline, when Lucard grabs her hip with his good hand, trying to drag her forward and onto him. "Wait," she mumbles, and with a silent sigh, she rips the crotch out of her leggings.

I cannot believe this is the second time in two days that I'm not properly dressed for sex, she fumes. *I really should know better by now!* She glares at the soon-to-be-vampire, blaming him for the loss of her clothes.

I'm going to charge him for both pairs, she decides, then scoots forward in a position her body knows instinctively. She finds the angle easily, sinking down atop his cock with a groan. Her succubus power spins out, encasing them both, and Amberleigh knows that this part is dangerous for a healthy human, the few moments between her power and the moment she returns the creature's powers. Normally, she enjoys this time, relishing the look in her partner's eyes as they realize just how vulnerable they are in that space between what they are and what they will be again.

Now, though, she knows that Lucard's human body is on the edge, weakened by blood loss and abuse, so she puts a hand atop his shoulder and braces both of her feet against the wall behind the toilet, balancing her weight so she can get the perfect angle. She rides him hard, knowing that is what she needs to cum quickly. Despite the circumstances—the bathroom stall, the bloody man before her, her brother likely still waiting at the bar for her return, the low hum of people just outside the bathroom door—the familiar thrill rises in her belly, the excitement that makes her a succubus filling her as the pleasure mounts.

Lucard grunts, his one good hand gripping her hip, tugging her closer with each stroke, losing himself in the pleasure even as she drains his remaining energy. "Zounds!" he curses, his age showing as he forgets everything except the ecstasy Amberleigh wrings from his body, his spirit. She feels the start of her orgasm, the vampire power she has borrowed spiraling away from her and sliding back into the body it recognizes. As she crests

A Quick Refresher On Bathroom Etiquette

the wave and spills over, Lucard's power pours back into his body. As she comes down from the high, eyes blurred with pleasure, she watches the wounds on his chest close almost immediately, smooth skin replacing the ragged tears. A second hand grabs her other hip, his wrist healed, and Lucard moves her steadily up and down, not breaking pace as he comes back to himself.

Amberleigh is glad to let the vampire power go, the distant heartbeats in the bar fading away, the sense of other life forces receding to her normal ability to judge power levels. Lucard leans down to kiss her, his lips moving the way she knew they could from their brief kiss under the overpass as he regains both power and skill. Amberleigh surrenders to his mouth, glad that now she can enjoy fucking the vampire without worrying about him dying on her. It's not the evening she had fantasized about, but his body is hard inside of her, his mouth soft and passionate, and she loses herself to another wave of pleasure. When she surfaces, Lucard is kissing her neck, and she knows where this is going, recalling her desires with Tony the night before. She tips her head back, letting it fall to give him easier access, and he bites her with practiced ease. Pleasure floods through her, and she shudders atop him again, body vibrating with ecstasy as the vampire's bite provides its version of the satisfaction she

Discovered

normally gives her partners with her succubus power. The next time she opens her eyes, she is resting against Lucard's chest, his chin atop her head, her gasps the only sound in the bathroom.

"Little Holder," Lucard says in a soft voice. Her hair moves in the breath from his lips. "I believe I am in your debt."

Amberleigh rallies, sitting up despite the languid boneless feel of her body. She manages a kiss to his cheek, then simply nods. "I was promised a full night of pleasure," she says finally, finding her voice. "Though right now, I'm too exhausted to appreciate it."

"Another time, then," he promises, kissing the top of her head and giving her a soft smile. He glances down at his chest, seeing the state of his clothing, and frowns. "I will be in much better shape. I promise."

"You want to tell me what happened?" she asks, tracing a finger along the clean new skin where claw marks had been. When Lucard pauses, clearly debating the wisdom of sharing his experience, she scoffs. "You had one simple rule, Lucard. Don't die." She frowns at him. "That was close."

"I know," he admits, and Amberleigh is surprised at his honesty. The Lucard she met the night before would not have admitted such weakness. "As I said, I am in your debt, little Holder."

A Quick Refresher On Bathroom Etiquette

"I have a name," she reminds him, though she doesn't mind the nickname.

Lucard frowns at her again, running a finger down the line of her jaw, tracing her mouth. "Do you, then?" he asks, and she watches his face, wondering just how much he had noticed in his human daze. He seems as though he's about to ask her something, but then the bathroom door opens, and someone enters. Lucard stands immediately, lifting her so her feet don't show beneath the bathroom stall door. Spinning, he lifts her off of him and sets her atop the toilet, pausing for her to find her feet on the edge before he lets her go.

"Hey, anyone in here?" Ben's voice is firm, more annoyed than worried. Amberleigh isn't sure how much time has passed, but she knows that her brother cannot find her in a bathroom stall with a stranger who is still covered in blood. She rubs her own neck, finding a small amount of blood there, and checks her chest. Smears of blood cover her too. Without a word, Lucard hands her the tank top from the door, then begins buckling his pants and buttoning his coat.

"Just me, I think," he calls out. He shuffles a little bit, then reaches behind where Amberleigh hovers atop the toilet and flushes it. He hands her sweater over, and she jams it over her head, careful to wipe her hands clean on the remains of her brown leggings first. She twists her hair into a messy bun, not sure what it looks like. Lucard glances at her, nods, then opens the stall door, and exits, careful to let the door swing mostly shut on his way out. "Something amiss?" he asks amiably, moving to the sink to wash his hands.

Amberleigh can sense her brother's annoyance shift to concern. "My sister," Ben says without preamble. "She came in here with you?"

"Just for a moment," Lucard replies smoothly, and Amberleigh can feel the power flowing off him, soothing her brother into acceptance. "She helped me to the stall, then went to the ladies room."

"Oh," Ben says, his voice the distant compliance of a vampire's victim now. Amberleigh doesn't like the idea of Lucard compelling her brother, but she likes the idea of Ben finding her in a bathroom stall with a stranger even less.

"Come with me," Lucard suggests. "We will wait for her at the bar." Amberleigh hears the door close behind them, then releases a ragged breath. She hops off the toilet and exits the stall, checking her appearance in the mirror, trying to be annoyed at the state of her leggings, but glad that her sweater is long enough to cover the damage. It will be a chilly walk home, though.

Again.

What am I doing? She studies her reflection in the mirror under the fluorescent

A Quick Refresher On Bathroom Etiquette

lights. *Maybe Ben is right. Maybe I need something normal in my life.* Washing her hands and giving herself one more onceover, she decides to call Celia as soon as she gets home.

New Year's Resolution, she decides. *Normal dates only: no more vampires in bathrooms. No more Holding for a little while, and never again for vampires.*

She fixes her face, restoring the Amber that Ben expects to see, then heads out of the bathroom to face her brother, determined to follow through this time.

Chapter 8

Adam Driver vs Hugh Dancy

Amber lays on her couch in the small walk-up apartment, staring at the phone in her hand. It's the last day of the year, and she has spent the last week lounging in her favorite pajamas and binging the latest K-drama on Netflix, this one about vampires caught up in the tangle of reincarnation. Putting on a fancy dress to meet Celia seems like a lot of effort when she can just order in and continue her TV marathon.

Her phone buzzes again, and she sighs, swiping up to see the latest message.

[Celia: Bitch, get your ass in the shower and get dressed. I'm not asking.]

Amber chuckles, loving her friend even if she can be a bit abrasive. Celia Jacoby may be a mild-mannered English professor by day, but Amber knew her before she got the Doctor before her name, and Celia is a wild woman. That side has mellowed since their college days as roommates, but Amber has been delighted to see the wicked side of her friend emerge a little bit on the few occasions she has gone out with her and her new boyfriend, a fellow English professor at the college. Dr. Jack Spelling is good for Celia—and apparently his brother is the perfect guy for Amber to meet tonight to start off the new year.

[Amber: <sexy Korean actor.gif>]
[Amber: I'm busy.]
[Celia: You could be actually busy if you come out with us tonight.]

Amber frowns, narrowing her eyes as she imagines the expression that would accompany the message. She waits for the follow-up she knows is coming.

[Celia: Busy getting some.]
[Celia: <sexy Adam Driver.gif>]

Amber groans, hating that Celia knows about her secret crush. She knows that John Spelling supposedly resembles his brother, and he may not be as big as Adam Driver, but Celia has mentioned his curly hair. "You know, the kind you just want to run your fingers through."

Celia has mentioned Jack's hair several times since they started dating. Amber knows her friend loves to tug on a good head of hair. Amber can take it or leave it, satisfied with tugging on other things, but her experience is far more varied than Celia's. Her friend is human, and while she has had lovers, she doesn't need them to stay alive the way Amber does.

Amber's succubus powers are controlled now, but when she first manifested her abilities, it was awkward and desperate—and Celia had been there for her friend while she went through a difficult time. Celia doesn't know what Amber is, doesn't know that Amber requires sexual energy in order to survive, but she knows her friend is a fan of casual sex and has never judged her for it in all the years of their friendship since that first year in the dorm. While Amber can also absorb sexual energy from a crowd, it's not enough to sustain her for more than a few days, and she needs physical interaction at least twice a week to feel content in her own skin.

After Holding for Lucard, she expected to be hungrier than usual, but she returned to normal almost immediately. She wonders if it is because she only Held for a day—usually her contracts run longer—three days is normal. That first time with Gerard, she had Held for ten days–a mistake she will never repeat again. It had taken months to truly recover herself. Celia had been deep in her master's thesis by then, too busy to truly help her drowning friend—not that she could have done much beyond what she was doing now—cajoling her out of pajamas and off the couch into a date.

Amber squints at her phone, debating. She hooked up with an elemental demon on Tuesday night, so she's not desperate for companionship quite yet.

[Amber: <sexy Hugh Dancy.gif>]
[Amber: Only Prince Charmont can get me out of pajamas today.]
[Celia: More like Aiden from that werewolf movie you love... he's got that daredevil grin.]
[Amber: What about that dark tortured past?]

The phone blinks for a long moment, three dots appearing and then disappearing next to Celia's name, as if she is deciding what to say. A heavy feeling sinks into Amber's gut.

[Amber: I don't need any drama. I get my fill on Netflix.]
[Celia: Nothing like that. But ... there's definitely a story there.]
[Amber: Now you're trying too hard. You know I'm a sucker for a good story.]

Discovered

[Celia: Did I mention that he's smart?]
[Amber: His brother's a college professor. He has to be smart.]
[Celia: Come on. It's New Years! I need you.]
[Celia: I bet John will need you too.]
[Celia: Need you to sit on his face.]

Amber sighs, groans, then kicks her legs out and up, letting the blanket she has been snuggled under fly up over her face. With another moan, she gathers it up and jams it under her head, grabbing her phone again.

[Amber: Fine.]
[Celia: You won't regret it. John is really nice. Definitely your type.]
[Amber: I have a type?]
[Celia: Smart-sexy. Though he's not bad to look at either. He's your kind of drifter.]
[Amber: I'm not sure if I should be insulted by that. Drifter?]
[Celia: You love those mysterious bad boys and you know it.]
[Amber: <accurate.gif>]
[Amber: You know me so well. And now you owe me one.]
[Celia: More than one, and you know it, but who's keeping count? I teach English, not math.]

Amber chuckles, then sits up, putting her phone on the side table.

"Okay, Lougle," she says to her voice-activated system, "turn off Netflix and play me some shower music."

Chapter 9

Just a normal date, please

"Amber, this is John," Celia introduces the man standing to her right, "Jack's brother." All four of them stand in the busy lobby waiting to be seated at their table. The host has disappeared into the crowd of bodies, and Amber smiles at the new addition to their party.

"That's not confusing or anything," Amber comments, taking John's hand and shaking briefly. The man is handsome, clearly related to Celia's boyfriend but without the wire-rimmed glasses, sharing the same dark wavy hair, though Jack's is kept short and semi respectable compared to his brother's wilder locks. John wears a black jacket and white shirt, the lines clean and fashionable, the kind of suit that costs a lot to look casual, but he stills looks slightly disreputable—the kind of look that Amber loves.

A jolt of power rockets up her hand and arm at John's touch, and their eyes meet in instant understanding.

Oh fuck, there goes my New Year's resolution, Amber thinks, biting her lip as she imagines what she could do with this man once she gets him alone. Tonight was supposed to be a normal date.

But John Spelling isn't a normal human. She wonders if his brother knows. She raises an eyebrow at him, and he glances quickly at where his brother and Celia lean against one another, the picture of the happy couple. He gives a quick shake of his head—no, they don't know—and she grins, nodding quickly as she releases his hand. She turns back to Jack, a younger, cleaner version of his supernatural brother. "Do people confuse you two?"

Celia laughs, covering her mouth and studiously pushing up her glasses as she stares adoringly at Jack. "Tell her," she demands. She turns to Amber, a familiar smirk already on her lips as she shakes her head, short hair moving across her shoulders. "Listen to this bullshit."

Jack reaches up and runs a hand through his hair, sending the short waves into disarray. Amber has met Jack before, so she knows that his hair is a mop by the end of the day. She hopes her friend spends a lot of time tugging

Discovered

on it. Jack Spelling has hair that is made for twisting between one's fingers.

Standing in her black party dress, Celia has a satisfied smile that Amber is happy to see on her friend's face. Celia had been lonely for a long time before meeting Jack. In fact, Amber can't remember meeting anyone since Celia broke up with Kevin back in their undergrad days. She hopes Jack Spelling is better for Celia than that asshole had been—not that Kevin hadn't gotten what he deserved after the way he treated Amber's friend. He probably still wasn't dating anyone either. Jack Spelling better treat her friend right. The soft smile on his lips suggests that he is just as smitten as Celia, and Amber appreciates just how handsome the professor is when he smiles at her friend.

Amber glances at his brother. John Spelling isn't too far behind, though less polished, and she knows she's going to fuck him before the night is through. Probably several times, judging by the power she senses rolling off him. *I wonder what you are*, she thinks. *Other than insanely powerful.*

John smirks in her direction, and for a moment, Amber wonders if he heard her thought, but then he is watching his brother, and the moment passes.

"So, funny story," Jack begins, giving his older brother a knowing glance, "my

Just A Normal Date, Please

brother here is known as the Professor to all our friends."

Amber frowns, looking back and forth between them. "But you're the professor," she says. "You teach English at the college with Celia." She looks over at John. "You teach there too? Celia didn't tell me that."

"Oh no," John says, and his voice makes a liquid shiver run up Celia's spine. "I'm not a teacher at all. More of a perpetual student."

"So..." She lets the word drag out. "Why?"

"It started when we were kids," Jack says with a smile. "Everyone thought John here would be the one to go to college. He was always reading something or other, hiding in the library."

"And you? I always thought you were studious your whole life," Amber comments, thinking of her friend Celia's tendency to always have a book handy. Surely, Jack would have been the same way. "You're an English teacher!"

"Not until I got to college," Jack admits, narrowing his eyes at his brother. "I spent high school playing baseball and getting drunk. But then my dear brother over there decided he wasn't going to college at all. He was going to bum around the world and 'find himself.'" He air quotes the last words and pauses, shaking his head. "Our parents were devastated, so when I got into college on a baseball scholarship, I decided to hit the books instead." He glances at Celia. "I read a poem about a beautiful unattainable woman in my English class—and I was hooked." His girlfriend blushes, and Jack ducks down to give her a quick kiss on the cheek. Amber sighs, knowing how much Celia hates to be reminded of the baggage associated with her name. Celia must really like Jack to appreciate the comment instead of being annoyed by it. Amber smiles, then turns to John for the rest of the story.

"Our parents thought they'd remind me of what a disappointment I am by calling me the Professor all the time—and then our friends picked it up, too," John explains, his voice warm and friendly despite the story.

Amber laughs, covering her mouth as she grimaces. "Oh no! That's terrible," she says, "but also kind of funny."

"I go all the way to a doctorate," Jack complains, "and our friends still call him the Professor."

"You're *my* professor," Celia croons, and Jack puts his arm around her shoulder and squeezes her close, placing a quick kiss on the top of her head.

The host returns to their small group, nodding for them to follow him, and the conversation pauses. The restaurant is nice enough, decorated for the New Year's party to follow the dinner, and Amber steps in front of John when he gestures. She can feel his eyes on her

Just A Normal Date, Please

ass, and she is glad she's wearing the new dress, the pale blue just tight enough around her hips to show off her curves. Her long hair is piled into a respectable updo, and she wears a simple necklace, opting for fashion over protection tonight. She has left her mother's pendant at home sitting on the bathroom sink. She'll put it on again tomorrow when she gets home from the penthouse where she will bring John tonight, when she settles into the New Year in sweatpants and a fuzzy sweater and binges a new show.

Maybe the one about the ghost in the bakery, she muses. *That looked fun.* Until then, however, she will enjoy herself and this chance to get to know someone new. John Spelling is a mystery she's looking forward to unraveling. John pulls out her chair and gestures for her to sit, a gentlemanly move that she appreciates, and she gives him a warm smile as she slides into the seat. He sits down next to her, both of them facing Celia and Jack across the table.

"So," Celia says after the waiter takes their drink orders, "Amber is a therapist." She smirks at John. "You can tell her all your secrets, and she can tell you what it all means."

John chuckles. "All of them? A man has to have some secrets," he says. "Otherwise, there's no mystery." Amber raises an eyebrow, noting the second time John has seemed to read her mind. She pulls her power close, not that protecting her thoughts is something she normally thinks about, but she imagines her magic like a shield all around her body. Her interest in John Spelling doesn't decrease, so she knows he isn't influencing her mind and forcing her attraction. Not that he would need to. Celia called it—he's exactly her type—the kind of man she would like to spend more than one pleasant evening with.

She leans over, moving her body closer to him. "And you are attracted to mysteries?" Amber prompts, curious to know more about the man next to her. He smiles at her, the look filled with promise. "I suppose you would be, having traveled to find yourself. How far did you go?"

"Everywhere," he replies, and she doesn't miss the challenge in his eyes as he adds, "and yet I never met anyone quite like you. Why do you think that is?"

"That's because Amber is one of a kind," Celia answers, winking at John.

"Is that so?" John echoes, giving her a knowing look. "Then I count myself lucky to have the pleasure of your company."

"The pleasure is all mine," Amber replies. *And will be yours*, she thinks, letting go of her shield for a moment to send out a tendril of her power to caress his arm. He glances down at his arm on the table as if he can see her touch and bites his lip as he takes a deep breath and adjusts in his chair.

Just A Normal Date, Please

It's already mine. The words are crystal clear in Amber's mind, and she stares at him wordless. He is reading her mind, likely has been since they met. She has heard of power strong enough to put thoughts into another's head, but she has never met anyone so strong.

You're a witch, she thinks, then reconsiders. That doesn't feel right. She's met witches, and while John's power is similar to that, it's not exactly the same. And there's definitely more of it.

Close, his voice whispers in her mind. *But I think I'll leave a little more mystery between us for the moment.*

Amber looks across the table at Celia and Jack, hoping that their silent conversation hasn't been too awkward, but her friend is distracted by the waiter dropping drinks in front of them, handing out menus and reciting the night's specials. She turns her attention back to her friends and the pretense of normalcy, but a brush of power moves her hair behind her ear, and she gives Jack a welcoming smile.

I'm so glad I got off the couch for this. It's already worth it.

Chapter 10

Dirty dancing but never in the corner

By 11p.m., Amber is dancing close with John in the crush of bodies moving in the middle of the room. She has lost sight of Celia and Jack in the crowd, but she doesn't much care. John is pressed against her back, hips moving in time with the beat of the music, and his hands rest on her hips. She reaches up a hand to caress his face behind her, sliding down to his neck and holding him close. He leans down, nuzzling his lips against her neck, and a slow spiral of pleasurable power radiates from her middle.

She rubs her ass against him, pleased to feel his hard response, and she knows that while some of her enjoyment is from her succubus nature, this connection is more than magical. It's been a while since she's felt such a strong, instant attraction like this—not since her early days when she was still getting control of her abilities.

She wonders if they can find a dark corner, then catches herself before she grabs his hand and leads him away. They are going to need more than a dark corner for what she has planned, but not before she tells him what she is. Amber doesn't enjoy blindsiding fellow creatures by stealing their powers. Still, she will have to talk to him soon, before she loses herself in her need to have him.

John seems to sense her desire, and he pulls her into the circle of his arms. She finds herself facing him, the crowd pushing them even closer together, and without a word, he leans down to kiss her. It occurs to Amber to stop, that she needs to warn him of her Holder ability, but the words die in her mouth as their lips meet, and then she is falling into his power.

So much magic, she thinks, the touch of his mouth lost in the moment as her Holder ability begins to pull his power into her. Strength infuses her limbs, warmth flooding her skin, and her mind sparks alive with awareness. She senses John's confusion, the pause as he tries to understand what she is doing to him, but he doesn't pull away. Instead, he deepens the kiss, tongue sliding into her mouth, and even more power floods into Amber. She can

Discovered

suddenly feel everything around her—the dancers around them, the people in the street outside, the foundation of the building and its connection to the earth beneath, the ley lines running through the heart of the city.

Oh no, she thinks. *This is bad. Something is wrong here.*

"It's—" she manages to say into his mouth, but then her voice fails. *It's not stopping,* she thinks, trying to direct the thought at John. Her awareness continues to grow, that sense of connection to the entire world threatening to overwhelm her. He pauses, sensing her distress, and pulls away, looking down at her in confusion.

His mouth moves, but Amber can't hear what he says, the power singing inside her too much. There is a pop, and she disconnects from that source, her awareness beginning to shrink back into herself again. Except it doesn't stop with her. The rest of the people in the room fade until all she can see is John's face—his magic still a bright glow around him.

I took so much, she thinks, *and it doesn't seem to matter at all. How strong is he?* Amber has Held for powerful creatures before, but it's never been like this. Even for the witches she has met, their magic was fun, fluffy like a cloud, and certainly convenient for the time she kept it, but this white bubble of power makes her feel like she's going to explode.

"Have to ... give it back," she mumbles, feeling her body sag forward into him, her legs no longer able to hold her upright as the borrowed power pushes against her skin from the inside.

John catches her easily, scooping her into his arms and maneuvering them off the floor. Amber is aware of bodies moving out of their way, either because of his expression or the power he still carries. The music pounds along with her heartbeat, and she is sweating profusely, the power threatening to split her open.

I have to let it go, she thinks desperately. *But how? Maybe I can use some of it, just to ease the pressure.* She closes her eyes and tries to push the magic out of her body, thinking of it like popping her ears by plugging her nose and blowing hard.

There is a loud pop and a scream as the entire room plunges into darkness. The music cuts off at the same time as the lights, all of the electricity in the building going out at once. John continues to move, carrying her through the crowd, seeming unconcerned by the sudden darkness. A moment later, streams of light begin to bob around the room, patrons turning on their phone lights. Someone starts playing music on a phone, another person cheers, and people behind John nervously shuffle around, trying to locate friends in the semi-darkness.

Discovered

Amber takes a shuddering breath, still in John's arms, feeling slightly relieved but still uncomfortably full of power. The noise of the crowd fades as they pass through a doorway, and Amber feels herself being carried up stairs and through another door into a quiet, dark space.

"Lights?" he asks, his voice soft in the darkness. "I don't want you to hit anything in here."

"Sure," she replies, still fighting to contain the power. She isn't sure how she knows—this power is nothing like the other powers she has Held before—but suddenly she knows how to harness some of the energy, and she lets out another burst, pushing the electricity into the lights she can feel in the room. The overhead lights blink on, blinding at first, then the pressure eases another notch, but still too much, tight against her skin. John gives her a curious look as he sets her down on a black leather couch along one wall. She groans a little, her skin hot and uncomfortable.

"What do you need?" John prompts as he sits next to her, body close to hers, one arm around her back to support her if she collapses again, the other reaching up to touch her face as he looks into her eyes. Amber looks away, not wanting to tell him, suddenly shy in a way she hasn't been in years. They are in what looks like an office, a large desk and executive chair across from the couch she sits on, two chairs in front of the desk, presumably for clients. John doesn't speak, watching her, waiting for her to tell him anything.

"I..." She shakes her head, unable to finish the thought with all of his magic still running beneath her skin. "I need to get rid of it," she mumbles. His eyes narrow in confusion, and he tilts his head, studying her. He begins to glow a little, his magic reaching out to touch her, and she scrambles away from him. "That," she says, gesturing in his direction, encompassing the glow she can see all around him. "I need to give it all back."

"I see," John says, pursing his lips as he studies her with his human senses. "May I touch you?" he asks after a moment of scrutiny.

"Don't put any more magic near me," she tells him, hunching over her body where she is curled up on the couch corner. Her skin pulses, every part of her body aching with the strain.

"That's what you mean—too much magic," he says slowly. "You somehow drained some of my magic." He nods. "Fascinating." He sniffs, runs a hand through his unruly hair, and holds out his hand in her direction. "Take my hand," he tells her. "I can pull it back."

"No you can't," she replies. "It doesn't work that way." But she reaches out her hand anyway, not willing to ignore the offered touch, the tiny possibility of relief.

"Trust me," he says, and something warm blooms in Amber's stomach, the same warm feeling that allowed her to kiss John without explaining her power or how it works.

"I do," she says suddenly. "I'm an idiot, but I do."

"You are many things, Amberleigh Miller, but you are not an idiot," he says, and she moves her hand a few inches to rest lightly in his outstretched palm. The same jolt runs up her arm, but instead of more power flooding into her, overwhelming her again, she feels a pause, a connection, and then John's power is sliding back into him, the same way all powers fall back into their owners when she has an orgasm. She stares at him with wide eyes, this witch who somehow managed to circumvent her abilities, as she sinks back into her body with a relieved sigh. As the last of his power leaves her, she closes her eyes, takes a deep breath, then opens them, facing her companion with her mind sharp again. John does not release her hand, and she doesn't move it away, but she does uncurl from the corner, sliding over to sit properly on the couch.

"So," John says after a beat, "you want to tell me what happened?"

"It's a really long story," she replies, running a hand through her hair and suddenly wondering if she looks okay. She is still sweaty, though her body temperature has regulated, and she gives him a wry grin. "Not how you want to spend your New Year's, I'm sure."

Dirty Dancing But Never In The Corner

John squeezes her hand gently, then reaches up to tuck a stray hair behind her ear. "I can't think of anywhere else I'd rather be right now." He gives her a hard look. "But you look like you need a drink."

Amber scoffs. "Definitely. But not alcohol, not right now." She grimaces as a shiver works its way up her spine, her damp skin reacting to the cool air of the office. "Sorry to ruin your midnight toast plans."

"Coffee?" he asks, rubbing her back with his free hand. "How about a midnight coffee and pie instead?"

"You still want to spend time with me after," she gestures broadly to everything, "that? Definitely not my best work tonight."

He nods. "I definitely need to spend more time with you after this," he replies, his voice sweet. "Come on. Let me buy you a cup of coffee, and you can tell me how you managed to siphon my power like that."

Amber stares at him, not sure how to handle a man like this. She knows men, knows how they normally react to a threat to their power, but John is different. He's intrigued but not threatened.

With that much power, what could ever threaten him?

She stares at him for a long beat, assessing, then nods. "Okay," she agrees, "but you have to give me a bite of your pie."

Discovered

"Of course," John agrees, getting to his feet and pulling her up beside him. "So long as I get a bite of yours."

Chapter 11

Midnight coffee and pie

They are the diner's only occupants, so the waitress and cook linger on the stools along the counter, chatting as they watch the musical acts leading up to the countdown on the television. Amber and Jack sit across from one another in a booth by the window along the street, far enough away that their conversation can go unheard. Amber sips her coffee, still marveling at the feel of her body now that Jack has taken back his power. She takes a bite of apple pie, closes her eyes to savor the flavor, then opens them to study the witch-plus across from her.

Jack hasn't said much since they arrived, focused on his coffee and chocolate pie, and Amber smirks at him, cleans her fork with what she hopes is a sexy motion, then leans in for a bite. At the same time, Jack reaches his chocolate-covered fork over to steal a bite of her pie. She parries in defense, their forks clanking in mid-air over the table.

Jack raises an eyebrow. "You said I could have some pie," he reminds her.

"You can—but lick your fork first. You can't go dragging your chocolate all over my apples. That's just wrong."

"I didn't think you were the kind to mind a little mess," he comments, bringing his fork to his mouth to lick it clean.

"Depends on the mess," she replies, using her clean fork to snag a bite of chocolate pie. "Mixing food is not something I enjoy, especially not apples and chocolate."

"You just haven't had the right combination yet," he insists but lets it go for the moment. "I learn more about you every moment," he says, smiling when she lets his clean fork take a bite.

"This place has good pie," she comments. "You were right."

Jack nods, taking another sip of his coffee. "I like it here," he tells her. "It's open 24 hours, so I can come late at night for a snack."

"You bring many people here with you, then?" Amber asks. The question is light, non-judgmental, just something two new acquaintances might ask. The subtext is clear enough.

"Not in a while," he assures her. "And definitely none as intriguing as you." Amber feels her face heat up and wonders how visible the blush is on her skin. She's not normally subject to such things. Her succubus nature makes it hard to appreciate the small feelings—she normally goes right in for the connection and satisfaction sex can bring.

But Jack Spelling is different, somehow. She just can't figure out how.

"I can say the same about you," she says, settling down for a serious discussion. "I've never met anyone like you before."

He nods, as if that much is obvious, but there's more to it than simple arrogance. Jack Spelling is different—and not because he's a creature or even a witch. Amber has been with many people over the years—no one has ever done that to her body before.

"That's because I don't think there are many people like me," he admits, running a hand through his hair. "Though you are not so common either." He gives her a long look, assessing now. "I'm assuming demon," he says. "Probably succubus, given the reaction of everyone around us."

Amber nods, though this is not normally the way she reveals her nature to other creatures. "I'm not a demon, though," she assures him. "I have the abilities—but I'm still just human."

He narrows his eyes. "One of your parents then or farther back in the line?" he asks.

Amber shrugs. "I don't know," she admits. "By the time I was brave enough to ask, there was no one around to answer."

He nods, face falling in sympathy. "I am sorry to hear that. It can be difficult to be alone."

"Well, I'm not totally alone," she adds. "I have a brother—but he's just normal."

"Are you sure about that?" Jack asks, and Amber laughs. The thought of Benjamin Miller as any kind of supernatural creature is too far-fetched to consider.

"Uh, definitely," she tells him. "Besides, I started manifesting around 20, so I would have noticed if something happened to him around his 20th birthday."

"Does he know about your abilities?" Jack asks.

Amber frowns. "Of course not. It's hardly something you tell a big brother!"

"So you hid it from him, then? Why is it not possible that he did the same?"

Her frown deepens and she takes another sip of coffee, recalling the way the woman at the bar had been stalking Ben when she arrived, thinking of other people drawn to her brother like flies, seeming unable to avoid the circle of his reach. She shakes her head, thinking of something else. "Ew," she says. "Just no. Not something I want to think about."

"It doesn't mean he's an incubus," Jack comments. "If it's just demon blood in your past, he could have manifested another demonic ability."

Amber sighs, taking another bite of pie and chewing thoughtfully. "You seem to know quite a bit about demon bloodlines," she says after a moment. "Is that something you studied when you were bumming around the world like Caine?"

He chuckles. "You know, *Kung Fu* reruns are available in more places than you would think." When she smiles but doesn't reply, clearly waiting for an answer, he sighs. "Yes. I studied many things—and demon bloodlines was one of them."

"So you said I'm not common, but there must be others like me, right?" Amber has met a handful of succubi in the last ten years, but she has never met another Holder.

"That depends on what you mean by 'like you,'" he says, taking a final sip of his coffee and eating the last bite of pie. After he swallows and wipes his mouth with the napkin, he gives her a hard stare. "You absorb other creature's powers?" When Amber nods, he continues, "With a touch?"

She looks down at the table. "With a kiss," she mumbles, then finishes her coffee.

"Amazing," he says. "That must make life as a succubus ... interesting." He shakes his head. "It must come as a shock to creatures that first time."

"Normally, I tell them first," she defends, hoping he can forgive her. "Normally, I have a whole conversation about it."

"What—every time?" he asks. "That sounds exhausting. What about spontaneity?"

"What about not wanting to drain someone's life force with a kiss?" she responds, frowning at his casual treatment of her powers.

"Can you?" he asks, leaning in.

"A human, yes," she answers, thinking of those awkward college days when she thought she had accidentally hooked up with a guy who'd been roofied. It took her a few times before she realized that she was the roofie. "Not immediately, but in an evening, definitely." She sighs. "Makes it hard to see anyone more than once."

"But surely you can maintain relationships with creatures," he argues. "If you just take some of their power when you kiss, they should have enough to spare."

"Oh no," she says, reaching out to touch his hand, that same zing shooting up her arm at the touch, "that's not how it works at all." He moves his other hand, so it rests atop hers, twining his fingers with hers and resting their hands on the table.

"How does it work then?"

"Usually, I take *all* of their powers. Then I can ... Hold them for a little while."

Jack stares at her, clearly working through his knowledge of powers to find the proper category for her gifts. He tilts his head. "You mean you can tire out even creatures like us?"

"No. I mean I make creatures human," she tells him. "Not tired. Just normal."

"Fascinating!" he says, looking down at their linked hands. "But you can't do it with a touch—only with a kiss?"

She nods.

"Every time?" he asks. "Every kiss?"

She shakes her head. "No. I get a break if I just released a power. It's usually a few hours before I can do it again."

"Like a refractory period of sorts," he muses. John is nodding, face deep in thought as he puts the pieces together. "It's tied to your succubus abilities, then, if it's triggered that way." He pauses, realization sinking in. "So you don't ever just kiss a creature without warning them, do you?"

Amber shakes her head. She learned her lesson that first time with Gerard so many years ago, when a thoughtless kiss had sent her spiraling into the vampire's control when he realized how useful her gift could be to someone in his position. Vampires may be powerful, but there are things that ordinary humans can do—like going into any house, occupied or not—that he found incredibly helpful to his goals at the time.

"But a human…" he prompts, his fingers sliding slowly against hers.

"A human just has a great time and wakes up exhausted," she says. "That's safer, but I still don't do it often."

"How do you survive then?" he asks, and he is genuinely interested. There is no judgment in his question, merely curiosity.

"I have ... friends," she says awkwardly, thinking of Tony, and the handful of creatures she hooks up with when she isn't working as a Holder. They already know what she is, so the loss of their power for a little while isn't a shock. Some of them enjoy the feeling of powerlessness for a bit.

Generally, though, it's easier to sleep with other creatures when she is Holding for shifters, magic users, or fae, since she isn't in danger of stealing their powers—and she can sometimes pass as whatever she is Holding for, so they don't suspect anything even when her normal succubus power drains some of their essence. Even though it is the modern age, some creatures still hold backward views of succubi, assuming the power they drain during sex never returns. Vampires are harder, though, due to the need for blood, but she limits her time Holding for them anyway.

"Demons are easier," she explains. "Especially succubi and incubi because they understand what I'm doing. That's just ... refreshing."

"Can you make other demons human?" he asks. "Even sex demons like you?"

She nods. "Sure. As long as I'm not already Holding, I can." She grins. "It doesn't usually last very long with incubi or succubi though—they are more keen on the sexual energy than anything else, so it's harder to ... wait."

Amber waits for him to ask what there is to wait for—waits for the moment when he will ask how she returns their powers, but John is still studying her. She understands why his friends call him the Professor now, this single-minded attention to a new discovery. He shakes his head, fascinated. "And others?" he pushes. "Vampires? Shifters? Fae? Witches?" She nods at each word, even the last one.

"All of them," she assures him. "Normally, I can render them human for a set amount of time—usually we contract for a few days."

"And then, what? You give their power back?"

Amber bites her lip, wiggling her fingers. He releases her hand. "Mm-hmm," she says, reaching for her mug and finding it empty.

"How?" He pauses, then adds, "You needed me to take it back from you."

"Yeah, let's talk about that," Amber says, glad for the chance to push the discussion in another direction. She's a succubus, and she's never been ashamed of what she is, but she's not looking forward to telling John Spelling how she normally uses her power.

Because you know that as soon as you say something, you are going to drag him out of here and have your way with him, preferably inside your warm apartment, but probably frantic against a convenient wall along the way—or both, actually.

"Can I be super blunt and ask what you are? I've never had that happen to me before. You have a ridiculous amount of power."

John smiles, pride and a little bit of mischief in the look. "What do you think I am?"

"Definitely a witch," she says. "I recognize the kind of power—but there's just so much. A normal witch has a chunk of power, but I can Hold it easily enough. Think of it like a battery." She gives him a look. "You're like trying to jam all the power on the grid into a AAA battery. It's doesn't work—but it just keeps coming."

"That's because I am connected to the land," he explains with a sigh. He gives her a considering look, clearly debating something. Finally, he sighs, and shakes his head. "You trusted me," he says, taking her hand in his again. "I will do the same. How much do you know about the powers of a bruja?"

Amber considers, skimming her memory. The word is vaguely familiar. "Definitely a type of witch, but something about ley lines, too, and some kind of connection to the homeland..." she muses. "Is that what I sensed then? Your power doesn't end because you're tapped into the planet?"

John nods.

"Wow," Amber breathes. "That's amazing." She cocks her head at him. "I can't imagine what that was like when it first manifested."

John chuckles, but something dark crosses his face, an unpleasant memory perhaps. "I always had an affinity for magic. My parents know, though Jack doesn't, so don't say anything to him or Celia—wait, does she know?"

Amber scoffs. "Tell my super straight-laced, ultra-organized English teacher college roommate about magic and demons and creatures? No thank you. Celia just thinks I appreciate men."

"Do you?" he asks, a flirtatious tone creeping into his voice again.

"Some of them," she replies warmly, "and some women too. Depends on my mood—and who is available."

John looks around the diner, then smiles at her, a look filled with promise. "I am available."

"I hope so," Amber blurts, then pauses. "But that power of yours is dangerous. Can you keep it in check? I don't feel like exploding tonight."

"I can," he promises, "but what I want to know is how you normally return the powers you—what is it you called it? Hold?"

Amber nods. "It's what I started calling it in my head when it first started." She stops, then blurts, "You've traveled a lot. Have you met other people like me? Other Holders?"

John frowns, considering, then shakes his head. "I've met people who negate powers, like a dead spot in a room, but none who could absorb powers and then return them." He gives her a hard look. "You have a very valuable talent, Amber. People would give a lot to use you."

"I charge a lot," Amber tells him.

"Do many people know of your ability?"

She shrugs. "A few. Enough to keep me comfortable. And I know how to keep myself safe," she insists. "Besides, I can steal anyone's powers with a kiss, and my succubus power makes it pretty hard to resist kissing me. I'm not worried about it."

John nods, but his expression shows he is not entirely convinced. He lets out a slow breath. "Perhaps I've just been too many places where exotic creatures are captured and held against their will. It's made me paranoid." Amber smiles at his use of the word exotic—she hasn't thought of herself that way, but she likes the idea. Though he brings up a valid point.

"You're not wrong," Amber assures him. "Creatures can be dangerous. I have my ways of staying safe."

"Does one of them involve avoiding important questions?" he asks, giving her a pointed stare. "That is the third time you've turned the discussion away from the way you return powers."

Midnight Coffee And Pie

Amber sighs, shaking her head. She straightens, then gives him her best succubus smile. "Fine. I return powers with an orgasm."

John stares at her, eyes darkening, and she feels the desire rise in him, the need to finish this discussion so they can move on to more pleasant distractions. "How very intriguing," he says quietly, his hand stroking hers softly, little thrills of delight skimming along her nerves.

"I'd love to show you," she teases.

John looks around, sees the two employees still sitting at the counter, then swears. He releases her hand long enough to reach into his back pocket, retrieve his wallet, and pull out enough money to cover their bill and leave a hefty tip. Then he is tugging her up out of the booth, nodding politely to the employees, and leading her out the door.

Amber waves at the employees, glimpsing the TV countdown to see that twelve minutes remain until the new year. She hopes to be ringing it in with style—preferably with John pressed deep inside her.

Chapter 12

Empty streets and powerful magic

Amber and John barely make it around the corner before he has pressed her up against the cold brick wall for another kiss. Even though he doesn't need to, she can feel him holding his power in check, building a shield around his magic so she can focus solely on the kiss. Her power won't rise again for a few hours—she can do as she wishes without worrying about a repeat of tonight's catastrophe.

John Spelling is an excellent kisser, and his mouth moves against hers in a way that makes her knees weak. Amber relishes every sensation, very aware that she normally misses this part of the connection, overwhelmed by the absorption of a new power.

Empty Streets And Powerful Magic

After a long moment, the wind works its way up the bottom of her coat to chill her thighs — she learned her lesson and is not wearing the warm tights tonight — and she shivers in John's embrace.

"We should go inside," she mumbles against his mouth. "Do you want to go somewhere warmer?"

"Oh yeah," he says, and then both of his hands are inside her coat, his body pressed tightly against hers, and she loses herself in the feel of his mouth as he kisses her again. The cold vanishes as a cloud of warmth suddenly surrounds them both, John's magic easily keeping the winter chill at bay. "I'll keep you warm," he says into her mouth.

His hands have worked their way beneath her dress, one squeezing her ass as the other reaches up to caress a nipple through her bra. Amber is very glad that she dressed appropriately for sex tonight, her thigh highs and lack of panties allowing for valuable access to the places she wants Jack to touch. She moans against his mouth as his hands move against her skin, wanting more.

"You taste so good," he mumbles into her mouth. "I need more of you." He sinks to his knees before her. Amber expects the cold air to replace where his body has been keeping her warm, but she remains comfortable, his magic heating the air around them. John begins pushing her dress up, and Amber glances quickly around the street, making sure no one else can see them. This is far from her first time engaging in public indecency, but she retains enough self-awareness to look around. The street is dark and deserted. She sighs in relief, then moans as John's mouth finds her bare pussy beneath the dress, giving her a long luxurious lick. He pulls away long enough to allow a tiny breeze of frigid air through his magic to tease her wet skin, eliciting a squeal, then replaces the cold with his warm mouth. He continues for a long moment, allowing her pleasure to build slowly, deliberately, sensing her needs as if he can read her mind.

I think he can read my mind, she thinks disjointedly, caught up in the pleasure of the moment.

Sometimes, the soft reply whispers, and John's hand joins his tongue, pressing into her the way she likes.

Oh fuck yeah, right there just like that, she thinks, and the rest is lost in a general wave of desire as she lets the pleasure wash over her, his tongue and fingers bringing her to a slow echoing release that she feels all the way to her fingertips. Her body shudders against the wall, her succubus powers absorbing the orgasm, and she sags for a moment, encased in a warm glow. John holds her easily, bending down to tease her again.

Empty Streets And Powerful Magic

"Oh no," she tells him, rallying. She reaches down to grab his shoulder and lifts him to his feet. "I need you. Now."

"You have me," he assures her, but chuckles as she works at his belt, unbuttoning his pants and relieved to find a sizeable cock within.

"I will have you," she promises him, lifting a leg around his hip. His hand reaches for her ass to lift her the rest of the way, and she wraps her other leg around him, locking her boots behind his ass. "Now," she repeats.

"I assure you, I am at your complete disposal," he says politely, then leans forward, pressing her back against the wall and sheathing himself in one move.

Amber grunts, adjusting so she can press back against him, riding him as much as he plunges into her, each of them goading the other on to fiercer pleasure. He keeps one hand on her ass to hold her close while the other braces against her shoulder, then he leans down to kiss her again, stronger this time.

The push of power is subtle at first, a tiny echo of the torrent she knows he has access to. At first, Amber assumes her succubus abilities are pulling power out of him like any other lover, but she recognizes the feel of her Holder power soaking it in, draining his magic as they kiss, the feeling familiar and yet unexpected because she should be tapped out. Slowly, she understands that John is allowing her to Hold his power, somehow pushing her ability to the surface in a small burst of pleasure. He seems to sense when she reaches her breaking point because the influx of magic stops, replaced by a complete focus on the physical sensations flooding her body. For a moment, she is more than just Amberleigh Miller, more than a succubus fucking a powerful witch on a cold winter's night—she can see just how both of them are connected to everything around them, the world a web of power and desire.

Then she is cumming again, and the power slides out of her back into him, her nerve endings tingling with the rush of magic as it leaves her. She shudders against him, both in physical delight and in metaphysical ecstasy, this use of her ability new and fascinating.

"Oh wow," she moans against his shoulder long minutes later, after her body stops throbbing with aftershocks of pleasure. Opening her eyes, she realizes that they have sunk to the ground, her sitting atop his thighs with her legs still wrapped around him as he kneels on the street, their bodies still joined. "That was ... just wow."

"You're telling me," John mumbles against her head, his breath warm despite the hint of cold she can feel drifting up from the street beneath the magic around them. "Is it always like that?"

"You asking me as a succubus?" she asks, mumbling against his shoulder. "Sex is always fun for me, but that ... was something else." She kisses his neck, a soft nip on his still heated skin. "Pretty sure it was the magic. Your magic."

"I thought so," he agrees. "Our magic." He leans forward to kiss her again, slowly this time, exploring her mouth and starting a new fire low in her belly.

Amber's thigh muscle twinges, and she reaches down to grab her leg. John releases her mouth, and Amber grins up at him. "I need to stand up," she says, and after a moment of awkward fumbling and resettling of abused limbs, they manage to stand up. John buttons up Amber's coat, making sure she is covered completely before he releases the warm bubble around them. The air is cold, the wind whipping, but Amber doesn't shiver, her body still warm and satiated.

A buzzing in her pocket catches her attention, and she reaches in to retrieve her phone. Several text messages show it is long after midnight, the traditional messages from friends filling her notifications. She sees a handful from Celia and opens them.

[Celia: Where'd you go, girl?]
[Celia: Guessing you and John found a quiet corner?]
[Celia: Happy new year! <exploding champagne bottle.gif>]
[Celia: Hope you're having a delightful time!]

Discovered

Amber smirks, then glances at John, who has pulled his own phone out to study it. He nods, then flips it shut. Amber is not shocked to see that he carries an old flip phone. She sends off a quick reply to Celia, assuring her friend that she and John are enjoying the new year very much, thank you, and grins at him.

"You know there's this new thing called a smartphone, right?"

"That new thing tends to malfunction when it spends too much time near me and my magic," John admits. "Something about the 5G technology interacting with the ley lines. I haven't figure out why yet." He smiles at her, pocketing his old phone. "I will. Until then, though, this works well enough." He nods at her own phone. "Celia checking in, I assume?"

Amber nods. "I told her we were having a great time." She frowns at him. "What now?"

John rubs his hands together briskly in the cold, then takes her hand. "Now we go inside somewhere warm, and I take off all those clothes and we do this again."

"And again?" Amber prompts.

"And again," John promises. "Do you have a place around here?"

Amber pauses, debating. She could take him to her penthouse, but she doesn't want to. John is hers, and she wants to keep him away from the places where she meets vampires. Her walk-up isn't far, and though she

Empty Streets And Powerful Magic

never brings men back there, she suddenly wants John to see her real home. She nods slowly, the idea growing in her mind. She can see John sitting on her comfy couch, them drinking coffee from her old mugs, curled up under a fuzzy blanket.

"I do," she says, leading him down the street, already planning all the places she will have him in her apartment. "Come with me."

"Of course," he says in that sexy voice she loves.

Best start to a new year ever.

Chapter 13

Morning coffee and quality couch blankets

Late morning finds Amber sprawled in her bed, John Spelling tucked up against her back like a warm blanket. She moans, echoes of the night's pleasure still resonating through her body, and twists to see if he is awake. There isn't a ton of space on the full mattress for both of them, and Amber is relieved to see his open eyes as he looks at her, a warm smile on his face, his hair rumpled and his eyes sleepy.

"Hey," she whispers, her throat a little sore from so much grunting and moaning and squealing.

"Hey," he replies, his voice low and throaty, a sound that makes a small shiver run up her spine.

Morning Coffee And Quality Couch Blankets

"Coffee?" she asks, knowing that she always wants a hot drink first thing.

"Bathroom," he replies, releasing her and rolling to his side to sit on the edge of the bed. "Then definitely coffee."

Amber nods. "Cream and sugar?" She watched him drink coffee with both at the diner.

John nods, then sniffs, stretching his long arms overhead with a series of small pops in his spine. Unable to resist, Amber sits up, scooting over to press her body against his back, feeling the heat of his body through the thin t-shirt she wears. He reaches back to embrace her with a sigh, and they linger there for a moment, enjoying the other's touch. Finally, Amber sits back, relishing the sight of his bare skin.

"You want some shorts to wear?" she offers. "I have some boxers that will fit you."

John stretches again, then nods. "Actually, yeah. Don't want to risk drinking hot coffee in the nude."

"I got you," Amber promises, hopping off the bed to pull a pair of old shorts from the bottom dresser drawer.

"Of course, the succubus would have extra clothes handy," John says, accepting the shorts and stepping into them.

"They're my brother's, actually," Amber says. "I don't keep men's clothes here."

"You don't?" John asks, genuinely surprised. "How do they get home? I mean, not to imply that you regularly wreck clothing."

Amber flushes, realizing what she has just revealed. "I don't normally bring people back … here."

John glances around the small apartment, the comfortable furnishings, the casual atmosphere. "You go to their place then?"

Amber shrugs. "Not really. I have other places."

"Other places?" he echoes, getting to his feet. "Give me a minute, and then I want to hear about how you can casually mention other homes when you already have a Manhattan apartment like this one."

Amber bustles about the kitchen with a soft smile on her face, aware that she is quietly humming, happiness and satisfaction singing in her bones, making coffee as John runs the water in the bathroom. She knows she will be hungry for breakfast soon, but not yet. She likes to enjoy her coffee first, then decide on food after she's awake and caffeinated. When John emerges from the bathroom, his hair a little wet and curling around his face, she hands him a mug of steaming coffee, watching his face as he takes a sip.

"That's good," he tells her, following her to the couch. Amber curls up on one side, tugging the blanket over her bare legs in habit. John sits near her, pulling her legs atop his

Morning Coffee And Quality Couch Blankets

with a casual gesture that Amber appreciates. They both settle under the blanket, sipping slowly. "Can I ask about the necklace in your bathroom?" he asks.

Amber pauses, trying to think of what she left on the sink in there. "Oh!" she exclaims. "The silver medallion? It was my mom's."

"It's a powerful artifact," John says casually. "A protection amulet."

Amber sips her coffee, then raises her eyebrows at him. "Really? I know it's magical in some way, but I just figured it was the normal family heirloom variety."

"Someone went to a great deal of trouble to keep you safe, Amber," John says seriously.

"Why don't you wear it?"

"It's silver," she explains. At John's blank expression, she adds, "It burns vampires."

"And you deal with vampires often?" he prompts.

She shrugs. "No, but my last client was…" She takes another sip. "Do you really want to talk about this?"

"No judgment, Amber," he says. "I know what you are and what you need."

"Do you now?" she teases. "One night in my bed and you know what I need?"

John shakes his head, smiling. "I would never presume," he says, earning a sweet smile from Amber. He puts a hand on her feet through the blanket, rubbing her gently. "You can tell me anything. I want to know."

Discovered

Amber sniffs, takes another sip of her coffee, then cocks her head, considering him. "What do you want to know, then?"

John looks around her apartment, relatively spacious by Manhattan standards, though nothing close to the penthouse. "So you have many homes?" he prompts.

"A few," Amber admits. "Creatures have different needs," she explains, "so I meet them places where it makes more sense."

"Like?"

"Well, the vampires like the penthouse," she begins, and John chuckles.

"Of course," he agrees. "That makes perfect sense. They enjoy looking down on others."

Amber laughs. "And I have a few houses for the shifters and witches and fae," she continues vaguely, not wanting to flaunt her wealth, knowing that for all she now knows about John Spelling, she doesn't know him that well yet. "I told you that people pay well for my talents."

"Obviously. But you don't bring people here," he pushes, looking around and then rubbing her foot again through the blanket. "Why not?"

Amber blushes, then takes a long sip of her coffee. Taking a breath, she gives him a hard look, owning her feelings. "Because this is my home," she tells him. "Not work. And I wanted you here ... in this part of my life."

Morning Coffee And Quality Couch Blankets

"I am glad," John says, his eyes warm and inviting over the coffee mug. "Thank you for bringing me into your life."

"I don't know," Amber says. "I mean, I like you—a lot. But this can get real weird real fast."

"This?" he asks, gesturing between their bodies on the couch.

Amber raises her eyebrow at him, then nudges his crotch with her foot under the blanket. "Sex is one thing, John," she tells him. "Even Holding is one thing." She looks around her apartment. "But I would like to see you again … just for company … and that's something else." She gives him a hard look. "Is that something you'd like?"

"You know I want to see you again, Amber," he replies, "and I think you also know that I want more of you than sex and Holding."

"What do you want?" she asks, her foot moving more aggressively against him, smirking at the resulting hardness she can feel.

"Right now, I want you at least twice before I have to leave," John says, leaning forward to put his mug down on the coffee table. "We can work out the rest later." He tugs her onto his lap, then plucks her mug from her hand and sets it down next to his. "Because there will be a later." His hands return to her face, one hand touching her chin and the other smoothing her hair. "I want to see you again.

Discovered

You, Amber. Not just the succubus and the great sex."

Amber wraps her arms around his neck, leaning in slowly to kiss him. She waits for the quick jerk of his head that lets her know he is ready for her, but instead of the insulation she expects, he feeds his power into her again, slowly filling her up like an hourglass, the magic settling in the gaps inside of her. She pulls away after a long moment, relishing the taste of sweet coffee on his lips, then bites her lip, frowning. She doesn't want to break the mood, but she's had this conversation before, occasionally wanting more than a simple hookup from a partner. They all assured her that it would be fine—that her nature was fine—but it never was.

Amber likes John Spelling, definitely wants to see him again, but she has to be sure that he knows what seeing her as more than a succubus or even a Holder means.

"I'm a succubus," she reminds him, leaning down to trail kisses along his neck and across his shoulder. "You know what that means?"

"It means you can do incredible things with your tongue," John says, a small shudder running through him as she kisses his body. As she adjusts her hips, a hand snaking down between their bodies to tug him free from where his cock strains against the thin fabric of the boxers, he adds, "And other bits." He sighs as she slides down atop him, his cock filling her warm pussy, then bites his lip and leans forward as she begins to move slowly, riding him gently.

"It means I need this," she reminds him. "And I need it from different people."

John's eyes open at that, watching her face as she moves slowly up and down. His hand reaches out to wrap around her hip, trying to goad her to move faster, but she holds steady, keeping the slow pace as her power pulls the desire over them both. "I know what you are," he tells her again, "and I know what you need."

"Are you going to get weird?" she pushes him. "Sometimes, people get angry. Possessive." She rocks her hips at the word, reminding him of what she possesses.

His hands grip her hips hard for a moment, but then he lets go, hands sliding up to rest upon her shoulders, letting her ride him as she will. "Part of me will want to possess you," he admits. "But a bigger part of me knows better than to presume to possess a succubus."

She nods, satisfied with his answers for now. "A bigger part?" she teases. "Is there a bigger part of you?"

"I am more than just my cock," he reminds her, a tiny flare of power behind the words.

"I hope so," she tells him, leaning down to kiss him again. "I'd like the chance to find out."

"Definitely," John agrees. "We have an entire new year to try it out."

Discovered

Amber nods, kissing him again as she picks up the rhythm, seeking her own release. John lets her move as she will, watching her with rapt attention until she begins to cum, the power slipping out of her, dragging through her body like a wave through the sand of a beach, and she comes apart atop him.

"Right now," John whispers, breathing hard as he kisses her cheek, "you are mine—and it's enough."

Chapter 14

Cab drivers are the worst

An hour later, Amber is in the shower, body singing with satisfaction as she washes away the scent of hours of sex. Not that Celia will judge her, she knows, but because it's generally bad form to stroll into a restaurant reeking of sex at noon on New Year's Day. Though she knows she won't be the only one.

John left a little while ago. Celia confirmed that the Spelling boys meet their parents at noon on New Year's Day for a celebratory lunch, a tradition established when they were still children, so Amber and Celia will also meet for lunch—to talk about their plans for the year—and to debrief about the night's escapades, of course.

Amber dresses casually, not expecting to meet anyone she knows, opting for a long tank top under a warm sweater and jeans, her feet warm inside comfortable boots. She stands in front of the mirror for a moment, running through any possible reason why she might need to have frantic sex today and comes up blank. She's not seeing John again until tomorrow at the soonest. She's completely satisfied and doesn't need to refill her power with a stranger. She shouldn't need to sacrifice any pants today.

Heading for the door, she grabs her boring brown winter coat—the one that lives on the hook by the door in this apartment. Her hair is tied back in a messy braid that she tucks into a brown toque. She debates bringing her purse but decides against it, shoving her phone in her pocket and her wallet in her jeans. She locks up quickly, dragging gloves over her hands as she drops the keys into her coat pocket and heads down the hallway and the few steps to the street.

On the street, she recalls John's comment about her mother's necklace, the protection artifact, and contemplates going back inside to put it in. Frowning, she shakes her head. She hasn't worn it in weeks now, and she's been fine. Maybe she'll put it on again when she gets home later.

The day is sunny, though freezing cold, and Amber huddles into her coat, even though she is warm enough. She debates returning inside for her scarf, then changes her mind, knowing

Cab Drivers Are The Worst

that the scarf she was thinking of disappeared with Lucard Monteban—and she isn't in any hurry to see that particular vampire again any time soon. The money was deposited in her account—but she hasn't put it down on that house in the Mediterranean quite yet—something holds her back. Lucard hasn't contacted her at all or explained what had befallen him as a human.

Amber has decided that she'd rather not know, and the loss of a scarf—and some nice leggings—is worth never seeing him again. Amber would rather leave bathroom hook-ups in her past along with other college hijinks. She ducks her head and hunches her shoulders against the wind, walking quickly. The Star Cafe is only five blocks away, and she can endure a few minutes of cold air. Amber hurries, aware of the others on the street with her, but only vaguely. Her neighborhood is safe, and she is still lost in a cloud of satisfaction and joy at her night with John Spelling.

I want to see him again, she thinks. *I know it's greedy of me, but with so much power, he can stand it. He can withstand my Holder ability, and even my succubus power doesn't seem to drain him that much. Considering that the man is basically connected to a battery the size of the planet, I'm not shocked. Besides, I want to learn more of what he knows about people like me—well, sort of like me, if not exactly.*

Discovered

She continues down the street, pausing at the corner to wait for the light. A man in a dark overcoat stares at her for a moment too long, a familiar feeling—people stare at her often— and she looks down, not wanting to attract too much attention—a danger she always faces as a succubus. She begins to subtly adjust her face, tugging her hat down low as she slowly settles into her Leigh face. It's only a few more blocks to the restaurant, and she can return to herself when she gets closer.

The light changes and the man moves closer to her as they cross the street, giving her another glance as they enter the crosswalk. Seeing her new features, he blanches, clearly confused to see a different person from the one he had been studying, and he nearly stumbles in his haste to get away from her. Leigh sighs, knowing that she needs to pay more attention to her surroundings, especially if she's going to walk around as satiated as she is, practically brimming with sexual energy. And she's not even Holding right now. Reaching the other side of the street, though, she allows her thoughts to drift back to John Spelling and what he may know about her abilities.

Maybe I can learn to release powers at will instead of having to wait for an orgasm. Maybe the orgasm release is hardwired because I'm a succubus and that's my default—but what if I can learn another way? Not that the orgasm part is bad—but sometimes it would be nice to have the option. She recalls staring at the battered Lucard in the bathroom stall, wondering how she was going to cum with him in that state, and sighs. *Yeah, definitely handy.*

Two blocks farther on, she becomes slowly aware of people's attention on her again, but this feels different. She looks around, seeking the source. Three men and a woman stand in a cluster on the sidewalk a dozen feet in front of her, the woman standing just outside the open door of a cab, as if preparing to get in.

Oh, Leigh thinks, *she's just looking at me.* As Leigh watches, the woman lifts a cellphone to eye level and moves her hand in a telltale motion. *Wait, did she just take a picture of me? I'm drawing way too much attention.*

Leigh makes a conscious effort to pull back her succubus appeal, her magic no doubt strengthened by the good mood and satisfaction she feels. She feels her power tighten, then rush back into her. *Wow,* she thinks, *that was … fast.* Almost like her power had been running away from something, eager to sink back inside and hide.

She looks up at the group again, seeing how the biggest man has edged out from the street to stand about halfway across the sidewalk, his bulk blocking her path. She adjusts her angle to move around him, aiming for the space between him and the wall of the building, but he steps out again, blocking her entirely. She jolts awkwardly to a halt. He is big, easily 300 pounds and over six feet, a mountain of a man with a beard and a black cap wearing a black coat and jeans.

"Excuse me," she says.

He looks down at her, and a hint of a smirk curls his lips. She can sense the desire wafting off him, but it's not a sexy feeling. Warning bells begin going off in Leigh's mind, and she recalls John's warnings from last night.

I've been too many places where people with exotic abilities are held against their will.

"Excuse me," she says louder, darting to her left, planning to dip around the man that way instead.

"Miss Miller," a voice says, and Leigh freezes, the magic infusing that voice filling her limbs with heaviness. "You should come with us." She forces her head to swivel, glancing up to see the middle-aged man standing near the street and the cab, his eyes pure white behind his glasses. She can see the magic pouring off him, tendrils sliding across the sidewalk and draping themselves over her body.

Fuck this, she thinks, lashing out with her own power. The magic encasing her seems to retreat for a second, unsure how to react to the violence of her push, and Leigh uses the time to bolt, ducking beneath the arm of the third man, a redhead, who reaches for her. For a moment, her world narrows to a single point—her eyesight fading away, her ears humming, her skin feeling like has been dropped into a bucket of ice, and she falters, feet tripping somehow. She can feel that her body is off balance, but she can't see or hear her movements.

What kind of magic is this?

She fumbles two more steps before agony explodes in her head, and the world comes rushing back in, a huge hand gripping her hair and jerking her back off her feet.

"Help!" she screams with her suddenly returned voice, knowing that making a scene is her best chance at this point. "Someone help me!" The hand holding her head tugs her close with another jolt, and then she is looking up into the big man's face, the redhead close beside them both.

Perfect.

"You don't want to hold me," she whispers softly, pushing all of her considerable succubus power into the words, seeing her magic curl around the big man, pulling him into her control. She hasn't used her power like this in a very long time, not since she learned to control herself, and she doesn't like doing it, but she doesn't like getting kidnapped either. "You want to help me get free," she adds, and the giant pulls her close, then turns his body so she is between him and the wall, the others behind him.

"Help you," he mumbles. Leigh wonders if she has time to snatch his powers, if he has any. She's not sensing anything beyond raw physical strength from the man, and it's possible he's just a human—a really big and strong human.

He'll do, she decides.

"They're trying to hurt me," she whispers. "You need to help me." She feels her words sink in, and the giant turns around, pushing her behind him. She hears the thump as the redhead who tried to grab her takes the first hit, then crumples to the ground. Leigh risks a glance around. Surely, someone on the street is seeing this. Someone must have heard her scream and called the police.

But the people on the sidewalk are walking by the fight without seeing it. Leigh watches as a woman picks up her child, darts into the street around the cab, then steps back up on the sidewalk to put the little girl back on her feet, the two walking as if they didn't just move around four people harassing a woman in broad daylight.

More magic, Leigh realizes. *But who?* Not the giant currently in her thrall. She glances around the huge body to study the two remaining would-be kidnappers. The woman has stepped onto the sidewalk, her phone out of sight now, seemingly annoyed in her designer coat and matching hat. She is tugging off her gloves as the other man, the one with the white eyes, continues to mumble, his magic fighting with Leigh's to reclaim the giant, who keeps swiping at both of them with lumbering arms. Leigh doesn't know if

Cab Drivers Are The Worst

she can enthrall more than one person at a time, but this seems like a good time to try, so she reaches out to the woman, trying to catch her eye.

For a moment, it seems to work, the woman leaning toward her, eyes widening with lust, bare hand reaching out to touch her arm, but the next second, an empty space surrounds them both.

Leigh's power disappears completely, the shock enough to knock the air from her lungs. She feels her facial features shift back into her Amber face as all magic leaves her body. Gasping, she stares at where the woman's finger rests on the bare skin of her wrist between her gloves and the sleeve of her coat, and more of John's words come back to her.

People who can negate magic, she thinks, *like a big empty space.*

I don't know if you can hear me, John Spelling, she thinks, *but if you can, I need your help.*

The giant, freed from Amber's thrall, immediately glares at her, then bends down to pick up his fallen comrade. He moves to the cab, tucking the unconscious man into the passenger seat. The man with the weird eyes and honey voice nods once, then heads around the car to the driver's seat. The woman, her hand now wrapped securely around Amber's wrist, tugs her toward the open door of the back seat. Amber resists, struggling to free herself, but the giant grabs her hair again and moves her forward. Amber is tugged and shoved into the back seat of the cab, yelling the entire time. When the giant slams the door behind him, pressing hard against her where she is jammed in the middle of the back seat, the woman lets go. Amber immediately reaches out with her power again, but the driver turns around to face her, eyes swirling white now. His eyebrow raises slightly, as if surprised to see the subtle shift of her face, but he recovers quickly.

"You will not resist," he commands, and Amber feels the order sink into her bones, her power no match for his after being in that dead zone. "You will obey."

"I will not," she manages to say, but her body follows his orders, sitting complacently in the back seat as the cab pulls out into traffic.

"You will," the woman next to her says quietly. "Everyone does."

"Not me," Amber grunts.

"And what makes you so special, Miss Miller?" the driver asks. "Other than the obvious?"

Amber fights the urge to answer him, to spill her secrets to the stranger. *It would feel so good*, her mind insists. *Just let go and tell him everything.*

Fuck that, Amber reminds herself, biting her lip to keep the words inside. *You know better than to give in because something feels good*. The thought is enough to repel the magical

Cab Drivers Are The Worst

push, and though the man gives her another speculative glance in the rear-view mirror, he doesn't speak again.

"Where are you taking me?" Amber demands as they weave through the streets, heading to the West Side Highway.

"Oh," the woman says, as if she has just recalled something, "the Collector sends his regards. You are cordially invited to spend some time at his residence."

"Being kidnapped isn't exactly cordial," Amber comments. "Can't he call like a normal person?"

"The Collector doesn't call," the woman says. "He commands."

Amber snorts, unable to stop the scoff from escaping at the cheesiness of that line. "Some names," she comments. "He collects and he commands, huh? Sounds impressive. Does he conquer as well, I presume?"

"He discovers," the woman whispers, and Amber doesn't like the cold feeling that snakes up her back at the look on the woman's face. "And then he keeps what he finds." She turns to face Amber, giving her a long stare, filled with something like pity. "He'll definitely keep you."

"I am not to be kept," Amber insists, but then the driver whispers, "Sleep," and she feels herself falling, sliding back and down into darkness.

Discovered

I may have been discovered, she thinks blearily, *but I will not be conquered.*

Amber and John will return in *Captured*!

Author Bio:

Ali Whippe loves trying new delights, especially of the non-vanilla variety. Her obsession with naughty words and sexy situations is only topped by her need to push the boundaries in every possible way. While her XTC and Honey Pot series play with all things wicked and sultry, the Collectors series is her first foray into paranormal erotica, and she never knew the world of magic and fantasy could be so deliciously sinful. She hopes you enjoy the ride as much as she did.

More books from 4 Horsemen Publications

Erotica

Ali Whippe
Office Hours
Tutoring Center
Athletics
Extra Credit
Financial Aid
Bound for Release
Fetish Circuit
Now You See Him
Sexual Playground
Swingers

Chastity Veldt
Molly in Milwaukee
Irene in Indianapolis
Lydia in Louisville
Natasha in Nashville
Alyssa in Atlanta
Betty in Birmingham
Carrie on Campus

Dalia Lance
My Home on Whore Island
Slumming It on Slut Street
Training of the Tramp
The Imperfect Perfection
Spring Break
72% Match
It Was Meant To Be…
Or Whatever

Honey Cummings
Sleeping with Sasquatch
Cuddling with Chupacabra
Naked with New
Jersey Devil
Laying with the
Lady in Blue
Wanton Woman in White
Beating it with Bloody Mary
Beau and Professor
Bestialora
The Goat's Gruff
Goldie and Her
Three Beards
Pied Piper's Pipe
Princess Pea's Bed
Pinocchio and the
Blow Up Doll
Jack's Beanstalk
Pulling Rapunzel's Hair
Curses & Crushes

Nick Savage
The Fairlane Incidents
The Fortunate Finn Fairlane
The Fragile Finn Fairlane
Us Of Legendary Gods
So We Stay Hidden
The West Haven Undead

Nova Embers
A Game of Sales
How Marketing Beats Dick

Certified Public Alpha (CPA)
On the Job Experience
My GIF is Bigger than Your GIF
Power Play
Plugging in My USB
Hunting the White Elephant

Caution: Slippery When Wet

SHAE COON
Bound in Love
Controlling Assets
For His Own Protection
Her Broken Pieces

FANTASY, SCIFI, & PARANORMAL ROMANCE

BEAU LAKE
The Beast Beside Me
The Beast Within Me
Taming the Beast: Novella
The Beast After Me
Charming the Beast: Novella
The Beast Like Me
An Eye for Emeralds
Swimming in Sapphires
Pining for Pearls

D. LAMBERT
To Walk into the Sands
Rydan
Celebrant
Northlander
Esparan
King
Traitor
His Last Name

DANIELLE ORSINO
Locked Out of Heaven
Thine Eyes of Mercy
From the Ashes
Kingdom Come

J.M. PAQUETTE
Klauden's Ring
Solyn's Body
The Inbetween
Hannah's Heart
Call Me Forth
Invite Me In
Keep Me Close

LYRA R. SAENZ
Prelude
Falsetto in the Woods: Novella
Ragtime Swing
Sonata
Song of the Sea
The Devil's Trill
Bercuese
To Heal a Songbird
Ghost March
Nocturne

T.S. Simons
Antipodes
The Liminal Space
Ouroboros
Caim
Sessrúmnir

Ty Carlson
The Bench
The Favorite

Valerie Willis
Cedric: The Demonic Knight
Romasanta: Father of Werewolves
The Oracle: Keeper of the Gaea's Gate
Artemis: Eye of Gaea
King Incubus: A New Reign

V.C. Willis
Prince's Priest
Priest's Assassin